FEDERALES

Praise for *Federales*

"In his debut novella, Christopher Irvin deftly captures the frustration and futility of the Mexican Drug War. Part character study, part thriller, *Federales* reads as a brutally human parable that tells a story that is sadly all too real."

— Johnny Shaw, Anthony Award winning
author of *Big Maria* and *Dove Season*

"*Federales* is stripped lean as a body dropped in the desert, as unrelenting as the sun that beats down on it. In here, there's no concern for what's right or what's moral, only what's inevitable."

— Nik Korpon, author of *Stay God*
and *Sweet Angel*

"Christopher Irvin's *Federales* is an absolute gut-punch of a novella. The story of one man s search for redemption and justice within a Mexican system that has long-forgotten the meaning of either will haunt you long after the last page is turned."

— Todd Robinson, author of *The Hard Bounce*

"*Federales* is a sweaty, feverish sojourn into a fetid limb of the Mexican drug war, where sentiment, principles and fellow feeling have no place. Christopher Irvin's read will carry you swiftly through to the fitting end."

— Sam Hawken, author of
The Dead Women of Juárez

"Chris Irvin displays a rare gift for creating atmosphere in this slow burn noir thriller. *Federales* is sneaky good. A few pages in and you're hooked. A few more and you can't breathe. Essential reading from an outstanding new talent."

— John Mantooth, author of
The Year of the Storm and *Shoebox Train Wreck*

"Sleek and fast as a bullet, *Federales* brings the seamy and deadly Mexican underworld to life—and signals the arrival of a major new talent."

— Nate Kenyon, award-winning author
of *Day One*

FEDERALES

Christopher Irvin

Jan!
Thank you so much! Weird Noir
buds for life!

Published by One Eye Press LLC

215 Loma Road
Charleston, WV 25314

www.OneEyePress.com

ISBN-13: 978-0615916545
ISBN-10: 0615916546

Contents

for Jenni

Acknowledgements

Thank you to One Eye Press and Ron Earl Phillips, who published some of my first stories in Shotgun Honey, rolled the dice and took me on as an editor, and on top of everything treated this book like it was his own. I'm forever grateful.

Thank you to my writing group, past and present: Bracken MacLeod, KL Pereira, Errick Nunnally, Javed Jahangir and TJ May. Without you guys I'd be a lost cause.

Thank you to my early readers and those in the writing community who have provided constant support and friendship along the way: Jen Conley, Erik Arneson, John Mantooth, Ian Rogers, Kate Laity, Jan Kozlowski, Todd Robinson, Nate Kenyon, Christopher Golden, John Dixon, Meghan Arcuri-Moran, Beverly Bambury, Joe Clifford, Tom Pitts, Nik Korpon, Isaac Kirkman, Chris Leek, Terrence McCauley, Richard Thomas, Elizabeth White, Christa Faust, Duane Swierczynski, John McIlveen, Chris Roach, Jillian Jacobs, Joe DellaGatta, Sam Hawken and Andrez Bergen.

Thank you to my parents for your unwavering support and ability to listen over the years, no matter how crazy the idea.

Thank you to my wife, Jenni. Our life together has been an adventure full of exciting life changes, and I can't tell you how much I admire your spirit. I love you so.

"Freedom brings with it responsibilities and I don't dare fall behind. My long road is not yet finished—the footprint that we leave behind in our country depends on the battle that we lose and the loyalty we put into it."

– Maria Santos Gorrostieta, 2009

One

Marcos startled awake, the bitter taste of blood and stale saliva on his tongue. Opening his mouth to lick his dry lips felt like unwinding a steel trap, jaw throbbing over his aching teeth.

The dream had found him again, the one where he knelt sentry, nose pressed against an impossibly large concrete wall, hands tied, knuckles pressed together against his lower back, waiting. In his gut he knew there was something peaceful and bright, an earthly heaven just on the other side. If he could only catch a glimpse, he'd know the way. The sound of a rifle bolt driving forward caused him to start, to open his mouth wide. No, *wider*, and gnash against the rocky wall, ignoring the pain and the blood as he broke his teeth trying to make one last hopeless dent. A scratch that said, *I was here.* An echo of the pain haunted him.

Marcos rubbed his eyes, adjusted them to the gloom. Though the sun was just beginning to set over Mexico City, the building where Marcos clocked his time had been in the dark for the better part of the afternoon. Hidden in an alley on the western edge of the sprawl, the small office had few windows, and those it did have faced a concrete wall that only enhanced the weariness of the never-ending drug war. The building had served as a warehouse for a range of businesses over the years, most recently a confectionery. On occasion Marcos would find tiny crystallized candy skulls that still appeared new despite years in hiding. Rats scuttled about, searching for the group memory of a past paradise. On dreary days such as this, Marcos often found himself drifting off at his desk, a habit no amount of coffee could deter. Sometimes he'd wake and pace barefoot along the windows to feel the suction of his feet against the cool tile floor, to know they were awake and firmly attached to the ground where they belonged.

The location of the offsite was restricted to a select few, but Marcos knew better than to consider the building secure. Restricted or not, if it was documented in the Federal System, it was game. The cartels had lined enough pockets to own the Policía Federal's secrets for years to come. He'd kept his head down and had been fortunate enough to stay off their radar for most of his career, but if they wanted him, they could have him. He'd accepted this early in his career, but it still shocked him how easily it came with the territory. It wouldn't do any good to let depression and paranoia rise to the surface. He kept those buried deep down and to himself. And so goes the life of a federal in Mexico. He was used to the constant struggle.

He ran a hand through his thick hair, one of the few assets of his aged body he'd been able to maintain. Thoughts of Ana had kept him from focusing on his backlog of work throughout the day, his index fingers pecking away at the keyboard in spurts as he hunched over the computer, forming poor sentences for a poor report on a poor case. Nothing about it was good, and with every misspelled word came an increased urge to smash the monitor, walk out the door and never come back. It was a daily routine.

Unlike Marcos, his wife was unable to ease the tension brought on by the day-to-day grind of her husband's work. When newspapers reported on brutal deaths of law enforcement officers, she'd hole up in their apartment, change the locks, close the blinds and survive on bread and boiled water for days on end. Alcohol only made it worse, often turning her depression violent. Marcos had to call on the hour while away and leave her messages letting her know he was safe or else risk her hurting herself. The constant stress of ensuring her happiness and stability became a heavy burden weighing him down.

He was in a rare groove when the new captain's assistant slipped his freshly cut key into the front door. Marcos didn't notice him until he was in front of the windows, a shade darker than the outside world. The man was thin, his head and face shaved to perfection. His body held the posture of a nail. The room took on the smell of a hot iron left on for too long.

"It's quite dark in here to be doing work," the man said, gesturing to the ceiling. Four light bulbs had burned out, two were missing.

"It's always dark in here."

"Doesn't the screen hurt your eyes?"

"It's the brightest thing I see all day."

The man's smile lit up in the dark. He had energy. A

strange energy.

"Marcos Camarena, no?"

Marcos paused, index fingers at the ready. "And you are?"

"Antonio Villa. I'm assisting Captain Ochoa with the transition."

"Transition." Marcos snorted mucous into his throat and swallowed. The cold had haunted him for weeks. "Right, transition." His focus returned to his task on the screen.

Villa pushed off the wall and moved toward Marcos's desk. His steps held the swagger of newfound power—the ability to push and pull, to change. He licked a thumb and rubbed it against one of the thick stacks of paperwork that had long ago overtaken Marcos's desk, overflowing onto a nearby folding table. He let out an airy whistle.

"You should get a desk lamp."

"I'll put it on the list. I'm sure it will be good for morale."

"Speaking of morale," said Villa as he walked around the side of Marcos's desk. "It has become quite the ghost town in your unit since Captain Garcia stepped off the force."

"Really? Hadn't noticed." But he had noticed. Ten men from the drug unit, all veterans, walked off the job without so much as a goodbye the day Ochoa moved in. No warning, no farewell, just service weapon and uniform folded and left in the desk drawer. He should have been one of them. Now he spent most days alone in a bullpen built for twenty.

"Are you wondering why you are still here?"

"Should I be?" Marcos crossed his arms over his chest. Villa had his attention. It was late and he was tired of games. Politics was an arena he was never good in and preferred to avoid. Villa chuckled and leaned back against the desk, appearing to enjoy conversations that played with the rank and file.

"The word on the street is you are a dependable man, Marcos. I've read your file. Unlike many of your former colleagues, you do your job quite well. Maybe a little missing paperwork here or there, but hey, no one is perfect."

"What do you want?" Every word that spilled from Villa's mouth added weight to the mountain range of to-dos.

"Fair enough. It's getting late and I'm wasting your valuable time." Villa rubbed his nose and crossed his arms, mirroring Marcos. "Captain Ochoa would like to, shall we say, reward a few of the top officers for their hard work over the past year. These are trying times, no?"

"We are losing."

"That's exactly the attitude we are trying to combat. We make small successes every day. Look at Beltran Leyva."

"He was given up, worth as much to the cartels as this paper." Marcos selected a large packet, thicker than his arm and bound with a rubber band. "Surveillance reports? I don't even know where these are coming from." He slapped the stack back down, past any attempt to hide his frustration.

"Listen, I get it. I want to help speed this up and get you back in the action. Problem is, since Garcia decided to land himself on the front page of the news—"

"Which was bullshit. Garcia is a good man."

"Well, due to that incident we now have our own media camp outside headquarters. They are requesting action by Congress, digging for details on all of our operations."

"And that's a problem?"

"A big one. A group of young journalists, led by one particular annoying creature, are leading the charge, trying to make a name for themselves."

Marcos began to respond but cut his words short. He knew where the conversation was going. He'd made it through his fifteen-year career by not asking questions. But, sometimes too much weight on a man's mind can make him act foolish.

"Maybe it wouldn't be such a bad thing." *Foolish.*

Villa brushed Marcos off with a flick of his wrist and disappeared without a word before Marcos could blink. Marcos slammed his fist onto the desk at the sound of the door clicking shut, cursing himself for being so brash. Villa was a wildcard, and that struck discord deep within his chest. He thought of Ana and wondered what she would have concluded from the exchange, what unsolicited advice she would have prescribed when it went south.

Probably to get lost.

He called it a night, packed up and headed for a drink, the only thing that could ever make him forget.

Two

The **Cacto Camina** sat five blocks southwest of Marcos's apartment. Close enough to stumble home through a patchwork of alleyways, yet far enough he could flee there to let his temper cool after a passionate fight with Ana. At the base of the crumbling stairs, the door was wedged open, as it often was, to air out the musty smell of sweat, spilled booze and cigarettes that clung to the ceiling like a smog. More old fashioned than dive, the Cacto was as close to a cop bar as you would find in Mexico City. Now located in a basement beneath a string of restaurants—it had moved twice over the years for security—the Cacto had become a second home for the regulars, both local policía and federales, politics be damned. They knew the danger of gathering, but each had been in the thick of it long enough to have a friend or two on the other side.

A low jingle of mariachi filled the room, eating the silence until the raucous crowd arrived late after dinner once their families were put to bed and they could comfortably blow off a week's worth of steam disguised as more work. Marcos nodded to a few early birds and took his usual spot on the far side of the bar. A clock outlined in white neon advertising Cazadores hung high on the central support post—Ana's favorite tequila, with lime and a splash of soda. His stomach turned at the thought.

"Tio," he called out to the bartender as he sat. His uncle had seen him enter and had the first shot already poured, setting it and a half bottle of Mezcales de Leyenda down in front of Marcos.

"It's been too long Marcos. Your lady keeping you to herself?"

Marcos threw back the slug and they embraced over the bar. His uncle still retained an iron grip in retirement, though his hands were soft. He had been a local cop in the days when the Mexican Government paid the cartels to stay quiet, to keep their bickering to themselves. He'd retired when the money slowed and the cartels traded places with the law, taking the spotlight and putting the badge behind a mask in the shadows. Like Marcos, Tio did not approve of change, his stout tequila stomach a result of career-ending stress.

Marcos let a sigh hiss between his lips as he retrieved a cigarette from his jacket pocket. Tio struck a match before Marcos could fumble his butane lighter open.

"Tell me," Tio said, waving the extinguished match. "You know it doesn't do your heart any favors to sulk in your favorite cantina." Tio poured him a second round of the smoky liquor.

Marcos gripped the base of the shot glass with thumb and middle finger. "It's been a rough few weeks. A lot of movement at the top has me buried under paperwork." Tio laid a palm over the drink.

"You are a federal. Every week is a rough week. Truly,

what is the matter?"

Marcos pulled the shot out from under Tio's hand, drained the glass and set it softly back on the bar.

"Ana left."

"Shit. Serious?"

Marcos nodded. Tio snatched the Añejo Don Julio from a crate under the bar, grabbed clean glasses, and poured two fingers in each. He took Marcos's hand and laid it over the top of the glass, covered it with his own and leaned in close. "Enjoy this one, nice and slow. We'll talk when you're ready."

Marcos took a sip. He couldn't help but smile at the smooth taste. Tio was very particular with his personal stash, even more so when it came to family.

"See? Already feeling better."

Marcos nodded again, though this time it was more forced. He didn't feel well at all. He'd had a knot in his stomach since she walked out the door in tears, leaving him standing there with that indifferent look on his face like she'd come back; she always did. And she had come back, while he was at work, to collect her things, their memories. Left nothing except a t-shirt and pair of underwear she must have missed, buried underneath a week's worth of dirty clothes. There was no one Marcos could talk to about the real Ana, not even Tio. The pain and embarrassment of failing to properly care for her caused him to keep his cards close. As far as anyone else knew, Ana was just another victim of a law enforcement career. It had taken much from Marcos to try and keep her happy. So much that a part of him felt a guilty sense of relief at her departure, and he hated himself for it.

He took another sip. Unlike himself, tequila improved with age. He was quickly approaching forty, and the only thing age had done was add bitterness to the cocktail.

"Give it time. It could be worse. You could have others meddling in your misery."

"Like you?"

Tio guffawed. "*No*, like the whole country." He hunched low, close to Marcos, and kicked his chin out in a gesture to the back corner. Marcos began to swivel on the stool but Tio smacked him lightly on the shoulder.

"What do they teach you boys these days? No wonder you can't catch a fly."

Marcos brushed off the embarrassment. Who cared who he looked at? He knew the face of everyone who visited the joint. He composed himself, waited for Tio to find a chore and turned to look.

The man's hat was pulled low over his face and he hugged the table like a person lost at sea clinging to a buoy. The man took a swig of beer, exposing an unmistakable thin mustache. Manuel Garcia. His eyes were far gone, only capable of staring off into blurry nothingness. Marcos turned wide-eyed to Tio, torn between the urge to console the former captain of his unit and smash a bottle over his head for allowing scum like Ochoa to take over. He balled his hands into fists, the stress of the headlines returning.

Three months ago, Garcia had a heart attack while underneath a prostitute at a whorehouse in Xochimilco. The resulting surgery and media blitz put him out on permanent disability. Had he been setup to take a fall, make room for a new crowd at the top? Marcos didn't know, didn't necessarily want to know. But Ochoa, son of a high-ranking congressman in the PRI, had obviously been gunning for the position, and had a reputation for using anything and anyone to move up the ladder. Get on the bastard's bad side and all bets are off said the rumors.

Tio returned when Marcos began to stand. "Shhh. Sit, sit. I only use the man as an example. Let him be."

"He's drinking himself to death after major heart surgery. Look at him, he looks one step from the grave."

"Sometimes a man just needs to be alone with his thoughts."

"What about you, bartender?"

"If he wanted to chat, he'd sit at the bar. Prying isn't good for repeat business. We only see one side of the story, Marcos."

"The only side."

The men were quiet for a long moment, letting the mariachi guitar fill the uncomfortable void. Tio uncapped four beers from a bucket of ice and passed them down the bar.

"Remember your father's first shoot?"

Marcos scoffed. "I was three."

"We were so nervous waiting outside that bank, with our puny six shooters."

"You guys were a mess."

"But we thought we were the best." Tio tapped his head. "The bank robber ran out the door, right smack into us. Your father pulled the trigger and, BOOM, shot off the man's right ear." They both laughed.

"Then he crouched over the man and said, 'You should listen to us when we tell you to come outside next time!'" Tio's belly shook as he laughed, tears in his eyes. "His face was white as a ghost!" Marcos downed the rest of the brown liquid.

"Give me something that burns."

Tio snatched the cheapest bottle in the house and poured a generous shot.

"The good ol' days, Tio." Marcos threw back the shot, finishing it with a coughing fit. "Nice pick," he sputtered, trying to laugh.

"You should take a few days, Marcos. Get away from life in the city and clear your head."

"I wish. I'm under a mountain of work."

"The work can always wait. I still have the beach house out in Manzanillo. It's a little rough, but it's got a kitchen and a roof. Take it. Relax."

"I don't know. Let me think on it." Marcos took out a few wrinkled bills and placed them on the bar.

"No, no, no, Marcos."

"Yes, Tio, and thank you, as always." Marcos stepped away from the bar before Tio could stuff the money back in his shirt pocket.

"One more for the road?"

"Nah, I'll save it for home."

"Remember, you're always on the way up when you walk out of this hole."

Marcos took the steps one at a time.

Three

The temperature had cooled since he entered the bar. He hugged his body for warmth as he zigzagged his way toward his apartment. Thoughts of Ana and Villa returned, making him itch. He wished he were back in the bar, taking Garcia's place in the darkest corner and drinking until the memories vanished and sleep claimed him. He paused at the entrance to his apartment building, rubbing his keys, almost turning back. A man emerged whom Marcos had never seen before, young with a military cut, wearing a tight black jacket and jeans. Marcos caught the door. The young man ignored him, wandering down the street into the night. It was still early, plenty of time to go back and get in a few rounds to help him plan the rest of his life. Marcos thought better and slipped inside. If he was going to make a fool of himself, he'd do it alone. He was up the stairs to the third floor and in front of his door before he realized something was off.

The lock had been scratched, edges of the keyhole slightly bent. His training kicked in and he flattened himself against the wall next to the door. He drew his pistol and pressed on the door. It squealed as it swung inward. Marcos took a deep breath. He'd be a silhouette—

an easy shot—to anyone hiding inside. He brought the gun's muzzle up to eye level, ducked low and entered the room. Three steps in he popped up and flicked the light switch on. He quickly swept the kitchen but froze when he reached the dining room table. The item lying on its surface told him the apartment was clear.

On the center of the table rested the casing of a spent .45 caliber pistol round. The adrenaline drained out of his body. His focus shifted to a line of framed photographs of friends in uniform he'd lost over the years. There was no mistaking the message, the threat. It was one Marcos had delivered himself on more than one past occasion.

When white knights die meaningless deaths, martyred in a hole with fifty other headless bodies in the Mexican desert, the world around them becomes colored with gray—corruption not an attribute but a scale; no longer a stigma but the status quo. It was never a question for Marcos to take, only when and how much. He never considered himself to be a sharp federal, though his friends would say he was one of the best. Marcos floated for fifteen years in the Policía Federal, equal parts investigator and water cooler, following the motto 'the tall nail gets the hammer.' He learned early in his years on the force, you don't volunteer until you're 'voluntold.' Crossing that line with Ochoa was what started the trouble in the first place.

He closed the door, lay his pistol on the table and dropped into a chair, exhausted. The casing was cold, probably taken from one of the drums at the range. He'd be dead before he could fill out the paperwork to trace the round.

He pulled out his phone and stared at the blue screen for a moment, mulling over his options. Scrolling through, he selected one of the last few men he could trust. Tio answered after several rings. The action at the bar had picked up but Marcos knew the man could hear him.

"Tio," he said. "Looks like I'll be taking you up on that offer."

Four

Tio's property was more rusty shack than beach house—the outside dilapidated, the inside in need of a thirty-year makeover. There was just enough room for Marcos to drop his bags alongside the twin bed without having to worry about them becoming an obstacle late at night. A tight bathroom with a shower stall and a wet bar that doubled as a kitchen rounded out the frills. If he wanted a television, he'd be hitting one of the many bars north along with the tourists. Which had been his plan anyway, as he was never one to stay alone for long periods of time.

He slipped off his shoes and socks and lay them near the door. The hushed sound of the waves cut through the thin walls of the house. He left the door open to let the salt and brine sweep out the dust and strolled across the beach toward the surf, the sand massaging his aching feet. The muscles in his legs threatened to cramp with each step, exhaustion taking its toll from the eight-plus hour drive fueled only by roadside snacks.

He'd packed two bags after he got off the phone with Tio, filled mostly with clothes and a few memories wedged in-between layers. He took an Ambien and set several alarms, the third of which woke him up, still groggy, six hours later. He knew he had time, but that did little to convince his nerves. Full of caffeine, Marcos was out the door and past Toluca de Lerdo before the sun could fully pull itself over the horizon. Like many men before him, the thought to call in or leave a note never crossed his mind.

He glanced back at the rickety house. Warm Pacific waves rolled over his toes, but he couldn't help the uneasy feeling in the pit of his stomach. Surrounded by a grove of palm trees, Tio's house was isolated for miles. Marcos suddenly found himself missing the stress and the smog of the city. He'd never been this far from civilization without a team of other heavily armed federales keeping him company. It was shocking that the place hadn't been vandalized or reclaimed by nature. Perhaps Tio rented it out more than he cared to admit. That, or it really belonged to an ex-wife. He buried the thoughts in the sand. There was no point in running if he couldn't relax. His stomach growled. Good salty food and a few beers would make Marcos feel at home.

He changed into a loose button-down shirt, taking care to conceal his service weapon—they could come and take it, but he wasn't leaving his baby behind—in a small holster inside his rear waistband. He locked up, heading north in search of dinner and whatever beach vacationers called routine.

Two days later his cell phone died, but by then Marcos had lost himself in a potent mix of sun and cheap beer.

It was a full month before the past caught up to him.

Not the recent, but one he had long forgotten, dressed in a tailored navy suit and expensive leather loafers with tassels not meant for the beach. The man emerged from the shade with his hands hidden in his pockets as Marcos trudged his way up the beach, thoughts set on a post-lunch siesta. He watched Marcos for a good minute before Marcos took his eyes off the sand long enough to notice him. Marcos's body locked up, his throat dried like a squeezed sponge. He reached for his pistol, finding only his sweat-soaked back. He'd become complacent over the weeks. The gun collected dust under the bed. The man was short with a slight belly, a thick head of black hair and a finely manicured mustache. Marcos jumped when he removed a hand from his pocket to dab the sweat from his forehead with a handkerchief.

"Easy there, Marcos." The man slipped the handkerchief back in his pocket. "Don't you recognize an old classmate?"

Marcos scratched his head, sun-struck brain tumbling through years of faces. The man stepped closer, careful not to bury his feet in the sand.

"Salinas?"

"At your service, my friend."

"Dios mio, it has been twenty years." They embraced, slapping each other on the back.

"You are a difficult man to track down," said Salinas, adjusting his suit coat. "Abandoning your post? That's not the Marcos I remember."

"Yeah, well, times called for a change of scenery." Marcos extended an arm to the front door. "Come, what brings you so far from the capital? Políticos not playing nice?"

Salinas chuckled. "They never do, but it's a bit personal, really. Let's talk inside."

Marcos grabbed two beers from a Styrofoam cooler. They sat down across from each other in a pair of beat-up plastic chairs Marcos had scrounged from the beach. He left the door cracked to circulate the air.

Salinas took a long pull and began. "There is a small but very serious movement in the government to put a halt to the cartel's grip on our country. It started last year in the Partido Acción Nacional and has since spread to freshmen congressional members in the Partido Revolucionario Institucional."

"Why hasn't the public been let in on the big secret?" Marcos couldn't help the tinge of sarcasm. While he appeared shocked at the sight of Salinas, the truth was Marcos had followed the career politician for years through the media. Salinas wasn't the snake the Partido Acción Nacional made him out to be, but he wasn't exactly transparent.

"It's too dangerous until we get a majority to commit to sweeping change."

"Surprise, politicians aren't willing to put their families on the line."

"We're not law enforcement, Marcos."

"No, you just make the law." Marcos gulped a third of his beer, stared at the floor. "I am sorry, Salinas. All this talk is bringing back memories of what I am trying to escape."

Salinas nodded. "That's why I need you Marcos. When I said we weren't in the public eye yet, I only spoke for the majority of us. Does the name Eva Santos ring any bells?"

How could it not? The living martyr for drug violence was on the news daily, rallying the few with courage to stand alongside her as she exposed her mutilated body for the cause. The former mayor of a small town on the Mexican coast just south of Manzanillo, Santos had survived two assassination attempts, the first of which killed her husband and left her riddled with bullets. He kept the images to himself.

"I saw she is running for a congressional seat. The local news has been running her campaign ads."

"Yes, she has a lot of support around her hometown." Salinas drank more of his beer in an effort to appear at ease, a veil Marcos saw right through.

"She is going to lose."

"Yes, I am afraid so. When the vote count is certain, the committee will strip Santos of her protective detail. She and her daughter will be alone."

"Christ."

"There will be people working in the background, but I need someone I can trust."

"You want me to be her shield."

"Another pair of eyes and ears. Experience to get her to safety should the need arise. We can't have such a major voice assassinated so soon after an election."

"But six months from now is okay."

"You get my point."

Marcos stood and walked outside into the sun, whipping his empty bottle into the trees. "I left this all behind, Salinas. Why do this to me?"

Salinas stood in the doorway. "You can't live like this forever, Marcos, you're too young."

"Young." Marcos laughed. "I haven't felt young in years."

"I'll pay you double your rate with the Feds. We'll take it week to week. Who knows, you make this look good and maybe we'll be having a different conversation next year. Until then, this is important."

Later, Marcos would remember the gritty feeling of sand between his toes and wish he had dug deeper. But that was after it turned bad, like he knew it inevitably would.

"I'll think on it."

"That's all I ask." Salinas handed Marcos a new phone and a card with a number to contact him. Then he was off, down the dirt road and back to Mexico City where he could play his games.

A week later Eva Santos packed in her campaign and headed home, alone.

Five

Marcos cursed his father after he called Salinas and
took the job. He couldn't put his finger on it—
some kind of goodness passed down in his veins that he
couldn't purge, no matter how much he drank. It only
took two nights of not being able to sleep before he caved.

Marcos drove the Manzanillo-Colima along the Pacific coast, his pistol clean and back on his hip where it
belonged, providing little comfort. Both attempts on Santos's life had been drive-by shootings from cars packed
with assault rifles. He held the steering wheel with his
knees and uncapped his canteen. Just a little sip to keep
the buzz going, maybe cause him to jerk right and off the
cliff. He laughed out loud, an insane laugh from a man
trying to convince himself otherwise. Dark clouds raked
the landscape in the distance, signaling the end of the
vacation.

When he reached the outskirts of Tecomàn, the rain
hit like a drive-through car wash, challenging the ancient
wipers on his SUV to keep up. The few cars ahead of him
pulled over to wait out the storm. Marcos clenched the
wheel, hoping the dark stretch continued as paved road.

After crawling for what seemed like miles, the neon

blur of a gas station caught Marcos's eye through the windshield. He gunned it across the highway, tires slipping in the muddy median, stopping at the second gas pump, which had enough protection overhead to keep him dry as he filled the tank. He pulled out his new cell phone and dialed a number Salinas had given him. A man answered, instructing Marcos to stay put and wait for a red pickup truck.

Seconds after Marcos ended the call, lightning struck a transformer atop a telephone pole in the distance, the explosion showering the sky with sparks of electricity. He dug his nails into the steering wheel, mouth slightly agape at the site of the smoldering tower. More bolts crackled and danced near the blast, congratulating the first successful strike. Marcos felt the hair on his arms stand up, like the electrical charge from the storm was probing for its next victim. He steeled himself for the coming unease, the instinctual desire to throw the car in drive, speed away and never look back. There was still time to run, to save himself from the darkening clouds. But in spite of the storm, he feared an ounce of cowardice more than anything—that tiny voice that selfishly lingered in the back of his head.

Then the tempest caught up with Marcos, booming with thunder as he threw himself out of the car, seeking shelter in the small bodega attached to the station.

He paced the store to slow the rhythm of his heart. The heaviest of the rain passed quickly in a blur, slamming sideways into the store windows. Once calm, he still had time to put a few pesos in the tank and drink half a lemon soda before his contact and a friend arrived. The man wearing a black poncho over a maroon hooded sweatshirt and jeans introduced himself as Paco, Eva's brother. His friend, Alfredo, looked like he had been dragged off the street. His head and shoulders were soaked, his too-large shirt sagged exposing collarbones. Marcos reluctantly removed his car key from his ring and handed it to the kid. He grabbed his bag from the back of the SUV and stood with Paco, watching as Alfredo revved the engine and tore off into the storm. He rubbed his chin, wondering if he'd ever see the car again.

"The car will be safe," said Paco, withholding the details on where it would be housed. Everything was on a need-to-know basis. Security tighter, the situation more dire than he had encountered on the job. His mind was still out on the beach, but the seriousness of the situation echoed like thunder in the distance—it was close, but hadn't dug in yet. Marcos crammed into the passenger side of the cab with his bag on his lap. The engine sputtered to life on the second try.

"Do I need to place a bag over my head?" asked Marcos, grunting at his own joke. Paco ignored him as he put the truck in gear. They turned onto a side road and headed for the dark heart of the city, where the clouds had eaten the sun.

Six

Paco and Marcos exchanged few words during the short drive. Within a half hour they were in downtown Tecomàn, creating their own random maze as Paco drove in circles, stopping twice at bodegas for soda and Chiclets. Marcos reserved judgment and let him work. The path was more madness than method, but if anyone had been following, Marcos would have seen them. Paco made one last turn into an alley barely wide enough for the truck, stopping in a dirt lot under a blue tarp on the other side. He pointed across the street to a white door set into a lime green stuccoed wall, both covered in graffiti. A metal gate shuttered the shop on the first floor, bars on the windows behind. DENTISTA was stenciled in large blue letters on the face of the balcony above. There was nothing special about the second floor apartment, just another beige building with chipping paint. Bars secured an air conditioning unit to the window, the wall beneath stained brown with leaked fluid.

"Ring twice, they are expecting you," said Paco.

Marcos opened the door to the sound of rain striking the tarp. A waterfall ran off the right side courtesy of a forward-thinking engineer. Paco grabbed his arm as he stepped out.

"Thank you for your help, amigo. I pray all of this struggle is worth it."

Marcos nodded back. He didn't think the struggle was worth it. He'd been fighting it for too long, his lenses too colored to see through to the other side. Paco reversed down the alley leaving Marcos alone in the dirt lot. He walked to the edge of the tarp and stared across the street. Curtains were drawn behind barred windows on the second floor, dimming the interior lights. The sky gave no hint of letting up. Marcos would get a good soaking running across the street, but there was no other way. *What's a little rain?* He picked up his bag and held it overhead as he jogged across the street. He was pleased that it caught the brunt of the storm, protecting his head and most of his upper body as he splashed through puddles.

He shook his canteen to see if it had refilled itself during the drive—it hadn't. Cleared his throat and pressed the doorbell. Then, remembering, pressed it again. A moment later he heard the patter of small feet running down stairs.

Clara Santos pressed herself up close to the peephole, the image on the other side cloaked in shadow. Her mother had said they were expecting company.

"Clara," called Eva. Before she could intervene, Clara ratcheted the three locks and opened the door. She stood bewildered, her limbs shaking as her nose took in the scent of fresh rain and tequila cologne. The word *Papá* almost escaping her lips.

"Clara," Eva shouted from above, taking the steps quickly in heels, one hand on the wall, careful not to stumble. Halfway down she paused akin to Clara when she saw Marcos, his features at first glance a stunning reminder of her late husband. Marcos took a step forward into the light, breaking the spell. He introduced himself. Eva scolded Clara, swatting at her and sending her back upstairs before turning to her guest.

"I guess you are the backup," she said, her eyes soaking him up head to toe. Marcos became acutely aware of how rusty he looked. He ran a hand through his greasy hair as an afterthought, his chance to improve the first impression gone. "Already I see in you how far I've fallen."

He smiled, his cheeks blooming at the quip. When his attention briefly flashed to the bulge on the right side of her abdomen, she saw through the facade. "Curious?"

"No." His retort was quick and came off more harshly than he'd meant. "No," he repeated in a softer, apologetic tone. He'd seen the photos on the news—the scarring on her chest, arms and back, the hole in her abdomen where surgeons removed the majority of her large intestine. She'd displayed the wounds for all to see as an expression of her fortitude, her perseverance in the face of a heartless enemy. Eva, like the spirit of the Mexican people, could never be defeated. She extended her hand.

"I am entrusting you with my life, Marcos."

"I will do my best." It felt like the right thing to say but the words rang hollow in his ears.

"Come," she said. He followed her upstairs where she gave him the quick tour of the small three-bedroom apartment. The place had a temporary feel, with the exception of Clara's room. It was clear Eva had done everything she could to make her daughter feel like she was home and safe from the danger outside. The dirt-brown walls had been painted light pink and there were enough toys to keep Clara occupied for months. The bedroom somehow even smelled new, blocking out the spices from the kitchen and smoke-stained carpet. Clara played with a pair of brightly colored ponies, trotting them alongside the edge of her bed.

A small cot had been laid out for Marcos in the third bedroom, which doubled as Eva's office. She ran him through her daily schedule, meetings with local leaders in neighboring towns, speaking engagements with law enforcement. Every minute was accounted for in color-coded blocks. For a woman who should be hiding, she was doing her best to keep herself on the firing line. She had several cars at her disposal to keep her enemies guessing. Nothing close to the custom armored vehicles of her former political life, but Paco's work as a mechanic meant they would have access to more in the future. Future. She used the word freely, like it was guaranteed to be sunny. Marcos concentrated on maintaining eye contact.

"Come," she said, leading him back through the apartment to the narrow kitchen. It was typical—blue tiles covered the counter, interrupted with a gas powered grill, small refrigerator and sink. A beat-up microwave sat off to the side unplugged. She pulled two bottles of water from a new case on the counter and extended one to Marcos. He uncapped it and took a sip while looking around the room. Like most of the house, there was nothing personal except what the previous tenants had left behind: a cross mounted high above the window and beer magnets on the fridge. A metallic Christ figure slumped crucified against the plain wooden cross, somber eyes watching over Marcos.

"The water is poor here," she said, turning on the faucet, which moaned and released a copper colored liquid that looked much like dehydrated piss. Marcos ran his hand through the stream and licked his finger.

"Better than Mexico City."

She chuckled. "Many things are better outside the capital. Unfortunately water isn't one of them."

Marcos nodded and took another sip. The view through the window above the sink was obscured by heavy bars, like the rest of the house. He could hear the tarp flapping in the dark as the wind rushed down the street. He took a step back from the window, jitters getting the best of him, becoming acutely aware that the only thing visible from the street outside was the silhouette of his head. Everything was new and he desired to process it on his own time.

"We don't cook much food," she said, gesturing to the unused grill. "The gas is better conserved for the hot water. Paco has been making trips or we stop while we are out." She had stacked Styrofoam containers three feet high beside a trash can. Marcos realized they were the source of the peppery smell and wondered how high the stack would have to get before she thought to throw them out.

"What about Clara?"

"She gets fed at school."

Marcos took another sip in response. Food, another liability. It was the little necessities that always caught up with people. He'd seen more people murdered while getting their hair cut than he cared to remember.

"Refrigerator work?"

"It does."

"Good, we only leave this apartment to drop Clara off to school and take you to meetings. No reason to risk another trip."

Marcos let it hang there. It was a test. She was in command, but for her to survive he needed the reins, at least a portion of the time. Eva stared at him for a moment, as if she was deciding how to punish the dissent.

"Now look—"

"Mom," Clara yelled, interrupting from her room.

"Just a minute honey." She turned to Marcos. "We'll discuss this later."

"What about your bedroom?"

"It's the same as the others."

"Layout? Windows?"

"If we are to work together, live together, we need a bit of privacy."

"Privacy? Eva, if you think—"

"You get your food and I get my privacy." She turned and left to answer Clara's calls.

Marcos finished the bottle of water in two gulps. *Compromise? Not half bad for a politician.*

Seven

Marcos rose in the early morning hours, just as sunlight began to creep its way into the apartment. A first since leaving Mexico City, but once up there was no use in trying to go back to sleep. It was a Saturday—according to the schedule, Eva and Clara's day to sleep in—so he was left to his own devices. With the exception of the buildings across the street and the alley leading to the covered dirt yard, he was blind to the layout of the neighborhood. Eva might not take well to him leaving her and her daughter alone, but they'd been safe in the apartment so far, and it would be quickest for Marcos to move about unencumbered, map out the neighborhood without constant concern.

He pulled on an old pair of jeans and slipped his handgun into the thin holster on the inside of his waistband. The weapon's cold metal against his lower back made him shiver and he wondered how he had wandered the beach all those days, drunk and unarmed. He wouldn't have been caught outside unarmed for a second in Mexico City. He felt a certain sense of assurance reacquainting with the gun, though it brought a level of anxiety with it he would have preferred to have left behind. He ran a hand along his shirt, testing the concealment, and left through the front door, circling back along the side of the building. Other than a pair of mutts rummaging through trash, the block was quiet. A musty smell of mud and earthworms permeated the breeze. Across the way, a corner of the tarp lay crumpled in the mud, torn off its post by the storm. He traced the concrete wall alongside the shuttered first floor office, pausing to run his fingers over bullet holes that he'd been unable to see in the dark. They were old—a good soul had tried to hide them with a thick coat of paint—large caliber and from the messy pattern, looked to be from a rifle fired on full auto. The story behind the wounds mattered little. Marcos felt even less as he fingered the imperfection. Just another piece of the environment, like graffiti or a pothole. All in need of some care—more than a fresh coat of paint or an orange cone could provide.

At the rear of the building he found a rickety metal staircase, still slick from the overnight rain. It shook under his weight as he climbed, rust painting his palms. He doubted it could hold more than one person at a time. He paused momentarily at the second floor where the staircase ended at Eva's apartment. No direct access through a door, but three windows lined the wall, one for each bedroom. The thick bars would protect from a break-in, but someone could spray the length of the apartment with gunfire in a matter of seconds. He made a mental note, though there wasn't much he could do about it. All of the buildings had roof access for gas delivery.

The left side of the ladder from the second floor to the roof was twisted, exposing large bolts that had once attached it to the concrete building. He pulled hard on each side, testing the metal. Despite its appearance, the ladder adhered to the wall. It was less than ten rungs but, hell, it was his first full day on the job and he wasn't taking any chances. The need to understand the full layout of the building was a priority that couldn't wait.

He dried his hands on his jeans and made the quick climb. The roof of the building was lined with a two-foot high wall, holes cut in the corners as a poor excuse for drainage. The slight pitch of the roof caused one large puddle to form on the left side, though the morning sun was already making a dent in it. Chalk-like lines had been left behind as the water evaporated across the roof. Thick, knotted bundles of wire and a weather-beaten gas container brought power to the building. It was the same on every rooftop as far as he could see. Clumsily arranged and exposed to the elements. It reminded Marcos of the poorer areas of Mexico City—modern amenities extended to all people without process and regulation. It was a miracle it all worked. He shook his head. "Remember why you are here, Marcos."

The thick concrete wall provided some cover, but with three and four story buildings in close proximity, he wrote it off. The best protection they had was their anonymity in the neighborhood, and if there was any truth to the media's report of Eva's stubbornness in the face of violence, Marcos had his work cut out for him to maintain it. A seagull landed on the adjacent rooftop, eyed Marcos and clacked its beak as it strolled along the edge. Marcos's stomach rumbled. He missed the beach, the sound of the waves gently waking him for a late breakfast.

Vacation's over, Marcos. You've got a job to do.

The surrounding neighborhood was a faded mix of small shops and apartments. Though most of the area appeared run-down, the signs of care were easy to spot. Several people had already raised their shutters and were sweeping the sidewalk in front of their shop or chatting with a neighbor. Two young boys in Bimbo sponsored jerseys passed Marcos at a sprint, their fútbol cleats clacking on the pavement, kicking at debris. Whoever had found this place for Eva had done a good job. Sure, she would be recognized by most if she lingered too long, but the calm Marcos felt was something of a bygone age. Something he hadn't seen since he was a kid. Though as he walked the neighboring streets, he felt more and more like an intruder, a wolf hiding from a hunter amongst a flock of sheep. The grip of his gun chafed against his back. He moved to adjust it and stopped, stuffing his anxious hands into his pockets. He watched the faces of those as he passed nod and go back to work. What he wouldn't give for a bit of their reality. He could never be one of them, not with what he knew. He'd chosen to swallow the bitter pill long ago and there was no turning back.

Ah, if Tio could only see me now. The veteran would have slapped Marcos and told him to suck it up. A cup of coffee with a tequila chaser. Hair of the agave perro. You made your bed, no time to wallow in it. The shared misery kept the gears of law enforcement turning.

Marcos stopped mid-stride at the first sight of coffee. The cement exterior of the shop was painted in a thick coat of red, with only its street number for a sign. Smaller than a walk-in closet and open to the elements except for the graffiti-marred shutters that hid in the ceiling. An older gentleman with coffee bean skin and a gray mustache poured hot water over a filter full of grounds stuffed into a paper cup. As they waited for the coffee to drip, he turned up an old radio atop a pile of boxes behind him, bending the antenna until it seemed like it would snap off in his hand. At last it caught a signal and buzzed to life, bleating news of the past night's fútbol matches. The man licked his lips and let out a low whistle at the news of Guadalajara losing their second match in a row in the Primera División. As one of the most successful teams in Mexican history, anything other than a league trophy was a disappointment.

Marcos gestured toward the Bimbo poster nailed to the wall. "Not a good year for them." The man just shook his head. Guadalajara had fallen deep into the middle of the pack and fans had little hope of a rally.

"Maybe they'll catch Pumas."

At that the man broke into laughter as he tapped the filter on the cup, shaking a few grains into the dark liquid. Marcos had been a Pumas fan since he was little, back when the team was lucky to avoid relegation to Segunda División. His family had all been Pumas fans, but even so, Marcos had a thing for underdogs, teams that had to scrap for a win, play every game like it was their last. Now Pumas were in cruise control, enjoying the past few years winning with style. Between spending the majority of his time at work and the rest clinging to Ana, Marcos had lost interest in the sport. Didn't know the players, or the result of the latest game. If the man serving him coffee knew, he would have shamed him. Such is the life of a fan.

The old man handed Marcos the cup and shooed him away, but not before something changed in his eyes. Like he was seeing Marcos again for the first time, except taking a moment to place him, and not being able to do so, marked him as strange.

Marcos walked a few blocks, letting the liquid cool before taking a sip. The flavors were strong, earthy smoke bringing the world around him into focus. He concluded there was little concern with the neighborhood. As long as they minded their own business, people should leave them alone. It was the type of place where people didn't answer questions. Not because they feared the cartels, but because they didn't know who to trust. It had taken years for Marcos to develop trust, working sources for the tiniest scraps of information. He wondered what had become of them, now that he was unable to do the little things. At least he kept his best sources off the books.

Only food and boredom were left over as his number one enemies. At least Clara was years from becoming a teenager. As he looped back to the apartment, he stopped at another shop and filled two plastic bags with breakfast items. Based on the stack of empty take-out containers, he doubted Eva had pulled anything together for the mornings.

It didn't dawn on him that he'd completely forgotten the tequila until he was spreading his finds out on the kitchen counter. "Shit." He'd mumbled, but not low enough to hide it from small ears. Clara sucked air through her teeth and clicked her tongue. Marcos started, almost knocking the pineapple juice from the counter. "Jesus you scared me, Clara." He pushed the groceries away from the edge of the counter.

Clara stood in the entrance to the kitchen, barefoot in pink pajamas that were a size too small, ending at her wrists and shins. She shook her head as she crossed the room. "Mommy says you shouldn't swear, or use the Lord's name in vain." She nudged past Marcos as if he wasn't there and picked through the groceries. She smiled. "You can make it up to me though. What's for breakfast?"

Marcos scanned the contents of the bags, tangerine juice, eggs, beans, tortillas and sweet cinnamon bread, and shrugged. He was sure he had something in mind when he made the purchase, but now the goods looked like a haphazard buffet.

"Hmm?" Clara grew impatient, crossed the kitchen, opened a low cabinet and pulled out a glass. She paused and reached for another. "Would you like one?"

"Yes."

"Yes, what?"

Marcos couldn't believe he was playing this game, but he formed the words. "Yes, please."

Clara smiled at her small victory and returned with the glasses. A spitfire in the making. Marcos poured them both a generous portion of juice. She took a small sip and exaggerated a sigh, like you'd see on daytime television.

"I'll have some bread and then two eggs and beans." She drew back her shoulders, defiant in her simple request. Marcos tore off a hunk of bread and held it out on a paper plate, only to withdraw it as she reached for it.

"What do you say?"

She crossed her arms and stamped a foot, upset the tables had been turned. Still, she managed to squeak out a 'please' and snatch the bread off the plate before Marcos could react, running off to the living room and jumping on the couch. She clicked on the television and lay munching in the morning sun.

Marcos chuckled. *Letting a kid steal from you. You're getting slow.* He took another sip of the overly sweet juice and got to work familiarizing himself with the kitchen.

There was more hiding in the cabinets than he thought: a few bowls, two cast iron skillets and several pots of varying sizes. Even a small spice rack and jars of flour and sugar. The takeout had more to do with either lack of time or Eva's lack of skill in the kitchen. Maybe both, but based on the detailed schedule in his room, he knew time was tight. Burning on both ends. He'd been accused of the same thing, as most good federales were. Being good was more about sacrifice than anything else, and that meant less time with the people you love.

He got to work, putting the beans, salt and water in a pot. Whisked eggs in a bowl. He let them sit while the beans simmered. The sun was already beginning to heat the stale apartment air. He pulled the cord twice on the ceiling fan in the kitchen, whipping a breeze into the room. Opened the kitchen window a crack, drawing in the sounds of the city. Motors and horns from the weekend traffic. A news helicopter passed high above, headed north to some incident in the distance, the sound of its blades drowned out by morning cartoons. Clara kicked her legs, tearing strips of sweet bread while stock characters sporting exaggerated features scurried about on the screen.

Marcos poured the eggs into a hot skillet and watched them sizzle. His stomach barked at the scent. He hadn't eaten much since Paco had dropped him off.

Eva's bedroom door opened and she stepped into the kitchen, white heels in hand.

"What's all this?" She swept a hand through her hair. It was still wet, but not overly so.

"Clara was up. I thought I'd make some breakfast." Marcos felt less anxious in the presence of his old supervisors. Eva wore a light blue suit with a gray tank top underneath and an almond colored pendant that matched her eyes around her neck.

"You went out alone?"

"Thought I'd give you some privacy."

"Quick to be abandoning your new post."

"I'm better on my own."

"You sound like me."

Marcos abruptly turned back to breakfast. He forgot to buy butter and had to scrape a portion of the eggs that were stuck to the pan and beginning to brown.

"I didn't know I hired a cook." Eva dismissed the food, though Marcus caught a glimpse of a smirk on her face that told him she was pleased with his efforts. She was a politician after all and the best were adept at hiding their satisfaction. "Clara, get dressed, we are going to be late."

"Late for what?" Marcos laid out three thick paper plates and split up the eggs.

Eva shook her head. "Didn't look at the schedule this morning?" She slit open the package of corn tortillas with a fingernail and slipped two out. "Just this for me." Marcos finished with the eggs and added the beans. He'd scanned the schedule only so far as 'sleeping in.' Felt embarrassed momentarily at the slip.

"Come, we'll take it for the road. Though if Clara ends up wearing it, that's on you." Her devilish smile caught Marcos off guard. He couldn't tell if she was a professional mask or a flirt. He didn't have time to think, as Clara came running out, ready for the day's adventure, and he found himself juggling food and their belongings to the car. Donkey, cook, errand boy. Salinas had better come through on his end of the deal.

Eight

They found Paco snoring in a van parked across the street. At first glance, the beat-up vehicle looked like any other, but the heavily tinted windows were an unnecessary flair. From the mud he'd tattooed on the pavement, it was obvious he'd driven a similar route as the previous night—down the alley, spinning his tires through the swamp underneath the wind-blown tarp and jumping the curb into the street with an awkward, spiraling U-turn. To call it a mess was being polite. It was the kind of shit on the job that made Marcos want to strangle his former coworkers. The kind of shit that got a source followed home and gunned down embracing his kids on the front steps. So much for operational security. Eva rapped on the window and he jolted awake, quickly opening the door and apologizing for his lateness.

Eva gave her brother a peck on the cheek. "Cheer up, Paco. There is no need to apologize. We're all under a bit of stress with the changes around here."

She didn't look back but Marcos knew she was referring to him. The replacement. One man sent to do the job of ten. He let it slide, knew he was more of a meat shield than a security detail. But he still had a job to do. Clara snapped the tension, throwing her arms around her uncle's waist, hugging him tight.

"How is my little princess," he groaned as he lifted her up by her armpits.

"I missed you," she said, poking him in the chest.

"I missed you too, but we've got to get going, little sobrina." Paco opened the sliding door and let Eva climb across before sliding Clara into her seat. Marcos handed her a plate of food that she barely noticed, still tuned to Paco, and slipped her purple backpack in beside her feet. Paco tickled her knee and drew the door shut.

He shook hands with Marcos, palming his matted hair. "Ready for your first day?" Thick yellow stains occupied the pits of his shirt and his skin was covered in a patchwork mixture of sweat, oil and dirt. It looked like it had been weeks since he'd gotten a comfortable night's sleep.

Marcos tightened his grip and dropped the charade.

"You look like shit, Paco." His voice a harsh whisper. He prodded his plate of food into Paco's belly, the beans adding another blemish to his already oil-stained shirt. "You pick me up and feed me all these grandiose ideas of secrecy, and multiple cars and hidden routes." Marcos pointed to muddy tracks. "Should we post a sign out front?"

Paco looked away, his pride visibly damaged. He couldn't muster the energy to defend himself.

"Look at me, Paco." Marcos took a step forward, trapping the exhausted man against the car. "The name of the game is to fit in. We can't do that with tinted windows and lazy planning. If we're late, we're late. That's better than never making it." Marcos placed a hand on his shoulder. "We good?"

Paco took a deep breath, pulled himself away from the brink of tears.

"I'm driving. You eat this, and when you get home, you sleep. It doesn't do us any good to have you running around at ten percent."

Paco took the plate and moped around to the passenger's side, already taking a bite before he buckled in. Marcos knew he'd been hard on the man, but by the look on Paco's face he'd been yearning for someone to tell him to go home. Any excuse to take a day off and try to relax without having to worry about his sister.

In the back, Eva seemed oblivious to the exchange, focused on keeping Clara from wearing her breakfast. Paco directed Marcos to the edge of town, where they dropped him off at a gas station eerily similar to the one where they'd first met. Marcos let it slide. He'd given Paco enough to sleep on. For their limited 'security' to work, Marcos needed everyone sharp and on his side. Paco was one thing; Eva, he knew would be another story.

Nine

They shared little on the bumpy ride to Barinas, less than an hour's drive north over pockmarked roads lined with lime trees, their destination high above the horizon, built upon a hill bordered by lush green mountains to the southeast. Eva passed most of the time on brief phone calls, confirming and reconfirming participation in future talks. Organizing discussions around how best to combat the drug trade took little effort—pushing local politicians and key members of the communities to stand up and act upon their rhetoric was the real hurdle. It was easy to sit in a dark room and vent, but with almost weekly news reports of assassinations, few were willing to risk their neck for the cause. Those few voices that did rise up and present a threat were swiftly dealt their fate. Eva was the exception.

The small village formed a bustling neighborhood around The Church of La Virgen del Rosario, the location where the meeting was scheduled to be held. Marcos pulled over near the front of the chapel and stepped out, stretching his legs. Gray clouds overhead threatened rain, but the sun was doing its best to cut through, bathing the sand-colored stone walls of the church in white light.

Marcos didn't believe in signs, but if he had it would have been a blessing. The right half of the chapel doors had been wedged open, but it was too bright outside to see anything within. The level of care given to the flowers and trees surrounding the courtyard entrance to the chapel was impressive. There wasn't a single piece of litter in sight.

A mix of key players from smaller cities in Colima were waiting inside. Marcos held up a palm to block the sun while checking the surroundings. A two-story hexagonal bell tower crowned the church to the right of the chapel. The iron bars protecting the lower windows told a different story. Even such a pristine and historical place as the church was not safe from vandals.

After taking a long moment for himself, he opened the sliding door and Eva's heels clacked on the sidewalk.

"Child safety locks?" Eva rolled her eyes, turned back to help Clara out of her seat.

"I need you to stay put in the van for a minute while I inspect the church."

"The hell you will."

"The hell I won't?" He felt his cheeks blush, caught off guard by her reaction.

"Look, I'm sorry. I didn't mean to take that tone with you, but I'm going to be late."

"The time doesn't matter—"

"Not as important as my life, I got it. But I've sacrificed nearly everything for this cause and I can't afford to appear weak at this stage in the game." She angled her head back to prevent forming tears from disturbing her makeup. "When I lost the election everyone said I was next, but I'm still here and—"

A clang of bells from the tower drowned out her voice. Marcos checked his watch—eleven.

He smiled. "Right on time." He should be her shadow, follow her inside and at least let his presence be known. He should have done his homework ahead of time. Establishing himself now would only cause a scene and deepen the rift between them.

"Do what you've got to do," he said, after the bells had struck their eleventh chime. "But in the future, you need to trust me. I'm here for a reason."

"I fully appreciate your concern, Marcos." The two locked eyes for a moment before Marcos gave in.

"We'll camp just outside the chapel. Anything goes south, I'm two steps away."

He looked at Clara, hugging her mother's leg. Two steps away were two steps too far. If shots were fired inside the church he'd most likely arrive too late, but he knew the point was both understood and moot.

"Thank you." She took a deep breath, regained her composure and gave Clara a kiss goodbye. "Go play with Marcos. Mommy will be back soon."

Marcos leaned against the van and watched Eva enter the main chapel of the church. Without a doubt, the woman was bold. To Marcos, her level of courage bordered on stupidity, but he couldn't help his feelings of admiration. Part of him wished he possessed an ounce of her passion. He'd been in the weeds too long to muster much optimism. Only time would tell.

Marcos picked up Clara's backpack and led her over to a concrete bench. With the sun nearly overhead, it was the only spot where they could catch a bit of shade from one of the short trees. There was little traffic and those who did pass gave them little notice. He tried to relax, loosen his shoulders. He didn't have the energy to run an alert 24/7 one-man show. Sooner or later he'd burn out if he didn't pick his battles. Something about the sound of the birds told him it was going to be fine.

Clara unzipped her backpack and pulled out a thick coloring book and a small box of crayons, which she placed on the bench next to Marcos. She knelt to use the bench as a table, flipping through the abused book, past page after page of images blotted with blobs of color. If there was one companion in her life besides her mother, it was the coloring book.

"You've given that book some love."

"It was a present from Papá," she said, nodding as she concentrated on filling in a purse with maroon.

To that Marcos sat quiet with his hands in his lap. He was never great with kids, always clueless at crime scenes on how best to handle the aftermath of a parent's murder. You'd think they would have training for something like that; they did for everything else. He'd wanted children of his own when he was younger, jealous of the fathers who could take kids aside and play games or watch television to distract them from the horrors of the surrounding events. Deep down the kids knew something was wrong, but in those surreal moments all was forgotten. Marcos wished he could find some of that elusive magic now. Perhaps staying with Clara would send a little his way.

"That's a beautiful purse."

"It's Mama's." She colored the strap black, careful not

to touch the hand of the woman on the page. "She needs a new one."

"She does?"

"Yeah, she said so. She works really hard."

"Your mother works very hard. What color is her dress?" Clara stared at the page for a moment, slowly scanned her box of crayons as if she wasn't ready to color the dress quite yet.

"How about green?"

"Yellow," she said, selecting sunshine yellow and scribbling at the bottom of the knee length dress, her decision final. After a few seconds she switched to forest green and filled in the dress, the yellow imperfection going unnoticed. Marcos couldn't help smile. This was the magic he'd been searching for.

The loud bleat of his cell phone jolted Marcos. He'd forgotten he set the ringer on loud when he left for Tecomàn. He pulled out the cheap flip-phone, a 'gift' from Salinas. At the beach the phone had felt new, but under the overcast sky it appeared old and beaten, like a scar Salinas had passed between sensitive sources.

The caller ID registered as blocked so he clicked off the ring and let it go to voicemail, figuring only Salinas knew the number and if it was him, he'd call back. Last thing he wanted to do was get bombarded with Tijuana timeshares and free cruises. Pick up once and the industry pegs you as a mark. Had to even change his cell number once. Nothing like getting blasted in the ear by the sound of a ship's horn. Seconds later the phone rang again. He answered, waiting in silence for the other party to respond.

"Hello? Marcos?" Salinas spoke in a hushed whisper, cupping his hand around the receiver. He sounded like he was transitioning between a cave and a wind tunnel.

"Marcos?" He tried again. Voices in the background, but muffled. Nothing Marcos could pick up. He stood and stepped away from the bench. Clara finished the lady in the green dress, turning the page to an image of a girl playing fútbol.

"Hello, Salinas."

"Hey, there you are. Good to hear your voice. Thought I'd check in and see how things are going."

"Sounds like you need a vacation."

He chuckled, a dirty, grating buzz in his throat, too close to the phone. "Not everyone is keen on our little arrangement." The laugh echoed of information withheld from Marcos. This was not the same 'friend' that had visited him at the beach. "So…?"

"Things are good."

"And Ms. Santos?"

"Fine. She's in a meeting."

"Tecomàn?"

"No, outside the city." The words escaped before he could pause and think better of it. He mentally slapped himself. Salinas did not have a need to know.

"Ah, Barinas. Popular."

Marcos clenched his teeth. He placed a hand on his lower back as he quickly re-scanned all of the nearby parked cars and places where someone could be waiting to make the hit. A tingling sensation washed over him, paranoia attempting to burrow within his psyche, something he always did his best to avoid as a federal.

Stay away from políticos and you can sleep at night. Now he was working off the books. Seconds ticked by, adding weight upon weight to his shoulders. *MISTAKE. MISTAKE. MISTAKE.*

"Listen, Salinas, let's cut the chatter." Marcos glanced back at Clara. She'd stood up to sit on the bench, still coloring away. He turned back, lowering his voice in a curt tone. "What's your angle here? First you come at me as a friend and now you're leaving me hanging. What is really going on?"

"Hold on a second." The volume increased in the background. Three or so voices in muffled discussion.

"Hold on a second?" Marcos took a deep breath, ready to throttle the squat man.

"Look, I've got to go." Back to whispers.

"Sure. Call me when you've got some good news."

"Not much to go around."

"Yeah, well find some." Marcos slapped the phone closed before Salinas could disconnect and whipped it across the church grounds. It skipped on the pavement and landed in a shrub. A game was afoot and he was trapped at the center with a woman whose boldness outstripped his naivety. He should have worked at a shitty bar pouring beer and cheap tequila for the rest of his short life. Should have known better than to trust an old friend-turned-político with so many years lost between them. He retrieved the phone in disgust, cracked but still operable. No matter where this dance took him, there was a part of his conscience that would never let him leave these girls.

"Give that back!" Clara, her voice a bullet in Marcos's

brain. Three young men hovered over her, the leader of the pack holding her coloring book high in the air, flipping through pages, laughing. Marcos knew the type—teenagers who came from wealth, trying to be punks. He could tell by the look of their faux-roughed up expensive clothing. The leader failing hard at growing a thin mustache. Marcos stormed over to the trio, ready to unleash his pent up rage. Before they could get defensive, he ripped the book from the kid's hands.

"Get fucking lost. Now." Marcos balled his fists, waiting for a reason to rip into the three.

"What? Can't a guy do a little coloring with the lady?" The three of them laughed like it was the funniest thing they'd heard all week. Probably high on something. "Go inside to your mother." He gave Clara a nudge and she went running for the chapel door. Marcos stepped around the bench, patience a frayed thread of yarn.

"You three had better beat it. I'm seriously seconds away from ripping your throats out." His face flushed. He let his emotions seep into his words. The boys maintained their taunting smiles, no respect for the authority of an adult. The 'Stache stepped forward, almost nose-to-nose with Marcos. Pulled his shirt up to display a large handgun.

"You see this old man? Looks like you should be the one to get fucking lost." The two in back slapped a high-five.

In two quick motions, Marcos wrapped his left hand around the grip of the kid's gun, pulling him close, and whipped his handgun out from the small of his back, jamming it into the kid's forehead.

"You think this is a fucking game?" Marcos briefly locked eyes with each of the trio, freezing them in place, his teeth clenched so tight the words barely made it out. 'Stache's fingers wiggled. He was contemplating making a move. Marcos cracked him in the forehead with the barrel of his handgun, holding tight to the kid's waist as he wobbled. "BANG. You are dead, kid." Marcos was yelling now, on the verge of losing control. "I've got two guns on you and you're thinking of taking me on? I could pull this trigger right now and blow your nuts off. Save our country from whatever fucked up offspring you might bring into this world." He jerked the gun to make the point. 'Stache paled, his grin a distant memory, fear dripping from his face.

"Marcos!" He heard Eva call out but refused to look away. It took everything to not strike the teenager. Age mattered little; the kid was just as capable of violence, if not more so, than a man ten years his senior. The perceived invincibility of youth only made things worse.

And then she was beside him, her fingers wrapped around his arm, whispering at him to stop. "They're just kids," she said.

Marcos holstered his weapon and ripped the handgun from 'Stache's waistband, dropped the magazine and pulled the slide back, ejecting a round from the chamber. "Just kids?"

Clara pressed close to Eva, hugging her coloring book tight to her chest.

"What's the meaning of this?" An older man stepped forward from the gaggle of politicians that had streamed out of the chapel after Eva. Spitting image of 'Stache.

Even in his fifties the man couldn't get it right. Marcos looked at Eva, felt his anger drain out through his toes. Felt guilty, like he'd done something horribly wrong. And yet when he turned his attention back to the teens, anger flared underneath his skin.

"What did you do to my son?" the man said, jabbing a finger at Marcos. 'Stache turned on the waterworks. Marcos had seen better flops on the fútbol field. He and his buddies were just trying to play with Clara when Marcos attacked them and threatened to kill them. Clara tried to speak up but Eva shushed her. The act was pathetic, but the old man was buying it. Or was he? Marcos caught a glimpse of knowing, a clue the old man knew what his son was capable of, maybe even condoned. The conspiracy was a stretch, but something was off. He just couldn't put his thumb on it firmly enough to speak up.

The man turned to Eva. "You speak to us in threats. You're no better than your dog." He spit at Marcos's feet, took his son by the shoulder and walked away, his friends in tow. Each of the other politicians filed past, some shaking Eva's hand, most acting like they couldn't get away fast enough.

"And it was going so well," she said after the procession had passed. She looked up at the sky. The clouds had fully blotted out the sun. Somewhere in the distance a car's muffler rumbled like thunder. "Let's just go."

Ten

They drove in silence, Eva in the front passenger seat staring at the countryside as they sped south toward Tecomàn. Early afternoon and the sky was painted like the coming of night. Marcos didn't bother pressing her to sit in back. Could he have handled the situation better? Maybe. But he was pretty sure the meeting had soured before the presidente municipal's kid decided to make an appearance. He kept his suspicions to himself.

Clara sat slumped in her seat in the back of the van, exhausted from all of the excitement. Marcos envied her, wished he could just go to sleep and wake up back on the beach, a few more pesos to his name. Mission accomplished.

Halfway back the traffic became heavy, slowing to a crawl. Shortly past the town of Caleras, the line came to a complete stop. Eva furrowed her brow at the annoyance, dug through her bag for her phone.

Marcos checked the mirrors. Nothing out of the ordinary, just a long line of traffic. *Must be an accident.* He drummed his fingers on the steering wheel as the minutes passed.

"Can you please stop that?" Eva said.

"Sure." He was getting antsy. First day out and all he did was manage to make more enemies. He replayed his conversation with Salinas in his head. There was a larger game here, but until he knew more he wouldn't share his thoughts with Eva. He had his work cut out for him, and concerning her with conspiracy theories would only add another tangled layer to his job. He cleared his throat.

"You need to tell me more about these meetings. I admit I was unprepared for today."

Eva sighed, fixed a mistake in her e-mail and continued typing on her phone. "Read. It's all there in your room."

"Dates and times, but not context. I'm not paid to read. I'm paid to protect you." He came off more harshly than he meant, a spike in the temper he thought he left behind in Mexico City.

"I thought you were paid to cook my meals." She didn't look up. This was a game to her; she wasn't frustrated. Marcos thought he saw a smile in the corner of her mouth and he almost laughed. *Stop this, Marcos, you are getting paranoid again.*

"That kid was one dare away from hurting your daughter. How can you expect officials to stand for your cause if they can't even stand up to their own blood?"

"His son has ties to local gangs." Her jaw tensed, unsuccessfully attempting to block the flow of information. "I knew it was a long shot."

"You think this information might have been helpful for me to know beforehand?"

She nodded slightly, relenting her position. "Relax, it's over and done with." She pulled out a charger for her phone and slotted it into a plug in the center console. "Looks like police up ahead. Maybe an accident."

Marcos shifted the car into park, the wind buffeting against the door as he jumped out, rounding the front of the vehicle to the side of the road. Lights from several police cars flickered in the distance. There was still a good bit of space between them and the scene. Marcos couldn't make out much but it looked like a car was off the road on its side. He stood there for a long moment, letting the wind whip around him. The temperature was still hot but it felt good to stand. Police alongside the line of cars clicked flashlights on and off, their heads poking in and out of cars. They'd set up a checkpoint. The cars ahead of them inched forward. Marcos returned to the van.

"Is there another way into Tecomàn?"

"Not really. Other routes would take us hours out of the way." She finished adding a telephone number from a scrap of paper into her phone. "Why?"

"Police checkpoint up ahead." Marcos cursed under his breath. Less than a quarter tank of gas. Turning around wasn't an option. Eva stopped her work and looked up.

"What's the problem? I'm glad to see them out actually doing their job."

"You trust the police?"

"I'm trusting you."

Marcos studied her face, letting her words sink in. Her coffee brown eyes were warm despite their murky depths. And when she swept a length of hair back behind an ear, her beauty made his heart ache.

I'm trusting you.

"Do not take me for a fool, Marcos. What many judge as reckless, I deem necessary. I refuse to live in fear."

"But—"

"How can I expect others to follow in my footsteps if I become a ghost?"

"What about Clara?"

He'd hurt her, but he couldn't hold back. If he could only show her what he'd seen on the job, the torment of the never-ending war. She maintained her resolve.

"If I am to pass before we emerge from this dark tunnel then Clara will grow strong and better for having witnessed such passion."

Marcos nodded. It was all he could do to spare her grief. A car behind them tapped their horn. The line had moved ahead.

"If you trust me, I need you to get in back with Clara and stay there until we arrive at the apartment." He shifted to drive and closed the gap. "And from now on I handle the police. Gossip is a cop's best friend."

Eva pulled her things together and slipped through the front seats past Clara to the back row. Soon flashing lights bathed the car, and a man tapped on the passenger-side window. Marcos rolled it down, holding a hand up to shield his eyes from the blinding flashlight.

"Put the car in park, sir." He sounded inexperienced, statements verbatim from young cops fresh from training. "ID?"

"Yeah, hold on."

"Who's traveling with you today?"

"Just my wife and daughter." Marcos played the act with ease, handed over his driver's license. The cop took some time with the license. The photograph on the ID was close to a decade old.

"You're going the wrong way." The cop angled his light into the back. Clara shifted in her seat as the light passed over her face.

"Excuse me?"

"You're a long way from Mexico City."

"Vacation."

"For how long?"

"Ten days."

"Where?"

"Tecomàn," Marcos shot back, tired of the rapid questioning. "Why the checkpoint?"

Marcos's question interrupted the rookie's train of thought, causing him to stumble over his response.

"Traffic collision… hit and run type. Looking for the driver." He handed Marcos back his ID and regained some composure.

"And your wife, sir?"

"She's in the very back. Not feeling well." Marcos mentally crossed his fingers. His hopes were dashed by the sound of the handle on the sliding door.

"Sir, I need you to unlock the door." The cop backed up, taking a safe angle on the side door. Marcos heard the pop of the snap holding the gun in his holster. *Great, last thing I need is a rookie losing his shit and putting a few holes in the van.*

Marcos reluctantly released the child safety, keyed the unlock, and the cop slid the door wide, free hand on his still-holstered weapon. He swung the light over Eva. Like Marcos, she held a hand up to block the light from her eyes. Still, the cop lingered on her. Marcos watched his face, didn't like what he saw.

Recognition.

"You're free to go. Have a good night." The cop slid the door closed and began to walk away.

"Who are you looking for?" Marcos called, but the cop waved them on and turned to the next car.

Marcos was slow to pull forward, his attention on the accident. More police cars lined the side of the road in front of the checkpoint, blocking most of the scene from view, but as they passed Marcos got a good look.

A white van lay on its side, roof and sides crumpled, evidence it rolled before coming to a stop. Maybe the driver lost control, or the car blew a tire? But right as he turned back to Tecomàn and the drive home, he saw the rear of the vehicle—windows blown out, riddled with bullet holes. Startled, he almost veered off the road before jerking the wheel. He shook from the adrenaline dump, tried to concentrate on keeping the vehicle straight. Watched the hashed yellow centerline in his peripheral vision, eyes not on the road but on the hood of the van.

Their white van.

For a split second he pictured a copper casing balanced on the tip of the hood like an ornament. He blinked and it was gone.

Eleven

Paco **met them** in a parking lot on the east side of Tecomàn with a set of keys to a silver SUV. Marcos called him to switch up the cars after the checkpoint. The sight of the wrecked van had him spooked, though he kept the details of what he'd seen to himself. The checkpoint alone was reason enough for Paco to repaint the van and change the plates, but Marcos insisted they switch vehicles.

Afterward, Marcos drove them around the city, stopping once for coffee—and tequila—getting intentionally lost a few times before finding the central roadways and heading for the apartment. Enough time and space to know they weren't being followed and for Eva to receive some bad news. A high profile meeting with the Colima city council had been postponed indefinitely. So much for progress. Marcos was just pleased they made it home in one piece.

Eva kicked off her heels in the entryway and stormed up the steps, her anger at the council flared in the open space of the apartment. She had seethed quietly as Marcos finished his route around the neighborhood. Weeks ago the city's representatives had all agreed to stand up with her in public, provide her increased protection and denounce the cartels. Someone intervened and changed their tune. Marcos had noticed it right away, the tension in her voice when she received the call. The meeting was over before it had begun, a rinse, wash and repeat of their morning. Colima, the state capital, was a linchpin city. Without their support, there was no chance of the neighboring towns fighting back. Marcos heard Eva opening cabinets in the kitchen, rummaging for something she'd buried. In his room he took a long drink from his canteen—refilled with his latest purchase—trying to relax before heading up into the path of Hurricane Eva.

It was the first time he had seen a crack in her armor, exacerbated by the fact he found her filling a glass of red wine to the brim. It was the first time he'd seen her drink. A night of firsts. He watched her take three generous gulps before topping it off again. She remembered Clara mid-pour, setting the bottle down hard in a splash of red. Her daughter had crawled under the covers, already sound asleep. Eva closed the door to her daughter's bedroom and returned to the kitchen.

Marcos pulled on a jacket. The rain had held off all day but he didn't want to get caught in another downpour.

"Where are you going?" she said, teeth clenched on the rim of her glass.

"Outside, I need to make a quick phone call."

"Something you can't do here?"

"It's personal."

"Are you working behind my back?" Eva stared hard at Marcos. "You've been acting strange since the accident."

That was no accident.

He wanted to tell her, but it could still just be his nerves acting up from the call with Salinas. The van, the young cop—they might not have anything to do with them. "I'm just over-thinking, that's all." He zipped up his jacket. "It's been a long day."

"Yes, it has."

At the top of the stairs he turned around, her accusation nagging at his pride. Couldn't leave without a shot at getting the last word. "Anyway, why would I do that?"

"For the money."

"No," he said, though that wasn't true. He could always use more. "What are you accusing me of doing? Threatening the mayor?" Marcos scoffed. Eva watched him intently as he braced his arms against the doorframe, stepping back into the living room.

"You know my entire schedule in advance. You had the time." Marcos thought back on the cop who lingered with his flashlight on Eva; another observation he'd kept to himself. He should have capped the conversation and headed for the door. But the tequila had begun to buzz about his brain like an annoying fly, bringing old habits back to haunt.

"You're accusing me of somehow working for the cartels."

"You *were* a cop once."

"I was a *federal*. And if I were so corrupt as you say, I would still have a job." He should have dropped the conversation there and left the room. Instead, he said, "Maybe if you stopped and thought for a moment on what you are doing, you'd realize this is all a lost cause."

The room quieted as she finished off the wine. She whipped the empty glass at Marcos. It sailed over his shoulder, smashing into the wall behind him.

"*You*," she said, coming at him. Marcos braced himself, still as a statue when she slapped him hard across the face. She stood against him, her breasts brushed against his chest with each heavy breath, tears welling in her eyes. For a moment Marcos thought she might kiss him. Then she dropped her gaze to the floor, retreated to the wine bottle and her bedroom without a word. Marcos skipped down the steps. Like fighting with Ana, he always walked out the loser.

Outside the night air pressed him like a sauna. He took off his jacket and dialed Salinas. The call didn't go to voicemail, so Marcos hung up after listening to the whirring ring for half a minute. He redialed to the same result. While Salinas was proving difficult to find, a cantina was not. A block down the street, the quarter-lit neon sign of a small watering hole caught his attention. It had one window and was so dark inside Marcos almost tripped over a dog sleeping by the entrance. The only customer, he took a seat on a duct tape-patched wobbly stool and ordered a round of shots for himself and the bartender, and a beer to nurse. The rain came, pelting the thin walls of the building. Marcos finished the beer and pulled his jacket back on. Inside, the temperature began to drop.

Three shots, four beers and six phone calls later, Salinas picked up.

"Stop calling this phone, jackass." Not Salinas,

someone else. Not a voice Marcos recognized. Deeper and less articulate, belonging to a larger man.

"Who is this? Put Salinas on the phone." Marcos slipped off his stool, caught himself on the bar before crashing through the door and out onto the sidewalk. Stepped back into the doorway to avoid the rain. Even though the initial downpour had passed, it was still coming down at a steady pace.

"Listen to me you washed-up drunk..." But Marcos wasn't listening. He was watching the dog from the cantina as it bolted across the street, splashing in the puddles, sniffing the fresh smells loosened by the rain. Thunder rumbled overhead.

"Put Salinas on the phone," he repeated, but by then the man had already hung up. Marcos redialed, stuffed it in his pocket and let it ring as he walked back. Maybe if he waited long enough, someone would pick up.

Twelve

Marcos woke with a start from a jab in the face. Lightning arced through his brain when he blinked. His throat felt scratched raw. Clara stood next to him in her pajamas, pink ponies chasing each other in circles. She gave him another poke in the forehead.

"Morning!"

The high-pitched greeting was a knife to the eye. The remnants of the tequila in the canteen spilled onto his shirt as he pushed himself up.

"Shit."

"That's a bad word."

"Why are you still in your pajamas? What time is it?" The room was too warm for early morning. He squinted at the clock. "Damn it." he said. "Go get your mother. We are late." She pranced off. "Bad words, bad words, Marcos."

Last night's argument replayed as he rubbed the sleep out of his eyes. He'd screwed up. It didn't matter what he thought. He should have kept his opinions to himself, gotten her the protection she needed and let her go off on her crusade. Eva cursed in the bedroom and yelled at Clara to get dressed and ready for school. Marcos felt Eva's bare feet stomp toward the living room. She appeared in the hallway, her face a mix of frustration and disappointment. She had changed into a purple nightgown with white lace around the neckline before turning in. The scars on her left arm visible where the rifle rounds had nearly torn it off at the bicep. She ran a hand through her sleep-strewn hair. He saw the grace and passion he had been so quick to write off as ugly. Her strength emanated throughout the room. Entering her life had only brought along further suffering. Her row was tough enough to hoe without a washed up bodyguard intent on drowning her dreams. He didn't have the time to take it back.

"Get up, we're leaving," she said.

His apology came out as, "I'll get the car ready." But he didn't want to leave. He wanted to hold her and confess that he believed in her cause. She didn't need to hope for protection because he would stay and stand with her.

"Just clean yourself up. I don't want it to look like we slept in a cantina."

Marcos nodded. He'd throw on a clean shirt and be ready in two.

"Today of all days," she said, blinking back tears. "Sure going out on a high note, cowboy."

Marcos started to speak but she brushed him off with a hand and retreated to her bedroom. He clutched his head, massaging his temples and cursing himself for his attachment to drink. That's the last time you overdo it, he thought, knowing it was a lie before the words even formed in his head. Nothing changes overnight.

He gargled water in the kitchen and gulped down two glasses before changing into a clean shirt. He rolled his sleeves in front of a mirror. The beard he still possessed from the beach was beginning to look haggard. He decided he would shave when they returned, a gesture to Eva that he was pulling it together. Out of habit he slung his canteen over his shoulder. Walking out of the room he felt it jingle on his waist. Not today. He took it off and tossed it on the bed. Today was as good as any to turn the corner.

He took a seat next to Clara in the kitchen as she finished her juice box and granola bar. Eva emerged minutes later in a yellow dress, makeup and perfume doing their best to hide the exhaustion. She looked better than good.

"Let's go, let's go, let's go," she said, snapping her fingers. Marcos tossed Clara's wrapper in the trash and followed them down the stairs and out the door. The same as every other day, except it wasn't. He should be in the lead, doing his job as opposed to thinking about hurt feelings.

His thoughts were on Clara's new pink bow as she walked in front of him, holding hands with her mother. He wanted to say something nice, something to make up for his startled responses, but he couldn't find the words. He decided he would go shopping after the meeting, find her something fun before he picked her up from Sunday school. Maybe some ribbon or a new pair of shoes. Little girls love guns.

Guns?

No.

Thirteen

Marcos opened his eyes.

The permanent florescent daylight that flooded the hospital had made it impossible to sleep for what felt like days. Some doctor's trick to wake him from his coma and, once alert, prevent him from ever finding rest again. He shifted in the hospital bed, the IV tugging against the tape on the back of his hand. Watched the slow drip, drip of the bag for a minute until he could no longer stand the drip noise that replayed in his head. His muscles ached with each contraction, stretching shriveled tendons as he swiveled his emaciated legs over the side of the bed. The pace of the beeping machines increased as his pulse quickened, sending throbbing sensations the length of his body.

One by one, he ripped the sensors off his chest until the room was silent and the only sound remaining was the drip, drip he heard when he thought of the IV. It was all driving him mad—the smell of medicinal cleanser masking sickness, the layers of sour sweat coating his body, the constant itching under the bandages, the thick grime he felt in his mouth when he ran his tongue along his teeth. He clawed his fingers through the uneven beard that had grown in the wake of violence. Felt an intense urge to find some immediate sense of normalcy: a toothbrush, soap, mouthwash, anything.

He slid off the bed, one hand gripped tightly around the IV stand, the other drifting along the bed rail, shuffling his feet across the tile to the bathroom in search of release.

Marcos tried his best not to cut himself shaving, but the bullet lodged in his brain made his image in the mirror blurry and he stopped himself, setting down the straight razor before he could do any real damage. Not that it would have come anywhere near the pain he'd carried for weeks since the ambush, but he was tired of the blood. He wiped himself off and tugged at sweat-soaked gauze wrapped around his head, covering the staples that held his fractured skull together. Drool dribbled out the corner of his mouth. He sucked it back in, his tongue trying to savor the steak he'd been smelling since he got in the shower. There was no steak sizzling on his apartment stove, but no matter how hard he concentrated he couldn't communicate the fact to his brain. Nor could he communicate it to anyone else through spoken word. Spanish tumbled out in unintelligible slurs, and his English even worse. *Incommunicado*. A word he never thought he'd associate with himself. The doctors told him he would most likely get his speech back through extensive therapy, but he stopped listening when they pulled out their clipboards, pointed at charts and explained the time line in years. Marcos plotted in hours, much less days. Like a stage four cancer patient, years were a foreign concept.

He swallowed another Vicodin and braced himself on the sink for the coming tremors as memory of the gunfire rippled through his wounded synapses.

Marcos feels the whoosh of the round spitting the air over his shoulder before he hears the rattle of the AK-47 on full auto. The deafening sound of the weapon pointed his direction is unmistakable, a tequila jackhammer behind his eyes. *Too much drink.* Rounds cut into the SUV, its doors as protective as Jell-O for Eva and her daughter Clara, both already buckled inside. *I am driving them to school today. You are late, Marcos.* Marcos has the driver's side door partway open, his left hand on the handle. The glass explodes in his face. Eva and Clara are screaming. The man with the rifle is running as he fires, bullets spraying in Marcos's direction. *Sloppy.* The man is brazen, does not wear a mask, but even so, his face is a blur. There are more men like him following behind. Marcos's pistol is in his hands and it bucks as he puts rounds back against the assailants, five into the point man, whose rifle dips as he falls, pulping his own foot. The rest of the mag goes into the crowd behind him. Marcos ducks to reload behind the door, slipping a spare magazine from a pouch on his thigh. The air smells like fireworks. Eva is screaming. *Stand. Make this look good.* Marcos brings the gun up, feels his finger hug the trigger, then nothing.

Marcos shuddered at the sink. He'd experienced his share of firefights. Intelligence on the location of cartel members would be delivered to his unit and they'd spring into action, flooding the area with overwhelming force and killing without pause. A knee-jerk reaction to a high-profile murder, a político who needed to clean up a leak, or a rival cartel calling in a favor—it didn't matter and he didn't need to know. The reason for the hit was more elusive than the criminals themselves. When the dust settled, the federales would line up the cash and dope for the Lieutenant's photo op. After the cameras turned away, the evidence was taken back to headquarters where a portion would be missing the next day. Almost like rusty clockwork.

He wet a towel and wiped the rest of the shaving cream off his face. He'd lost so much weight over the past month, he hardly recognized himself. The IV bags kept him hydrated but his body had cannibalized much of his muscle in order to survive. He left the bathroom, his eyes on the cold tile beneath his feet.

"Marcos."

Startled, Marcos looked up at the sound of the voice. For a moment he couldn't place the suit. Then he remembered, *Salinas*. The man who'd hired him to guard the woman. *Eva*. Details came back piecemeal, in odd combinations.

In the few days since he woken from the coma, he'd tried to remember the moments before he was shot, but his memories were of sounds and scents—screams interrupted by the staccato of gunfire, clouds full of gunpowder and sweat. It was as if the injection of adrenaline had doubled as a memory eraser, eating up his thoughts, triggered at the sound of gunfire.

Salinas stood in the doorway, arms limp at his side. A giant of a man stepped into the room behind him, gave

Marcos a once-over. Salinas crossed the room without a word, embracing Marcos, squeezing his bones.

"You look much better, my friend," he said, observing the head wrapping. "When I first visited, the doctors didn't think you'd make it."

Like the others.

"And then when they called and said you'd pulled through, I couldn't believe it."

So you had to see it with your own two eyes.

The image was blurry, but Marcos remembered the sweet smell of cigars and the stink of cheap booze. The sound of Salinas's voice as he calmly asked Marcos, "What do you remember?"

Nothing.

He licked his lips—the mouth-watering smell of the steak vanished. The pain meds gave him cotton mouth.

"Please sit down, sit down." Salinas stepped back so Marcos could have a seat on the bed. "Juan, the bag," he said, gesturing to the giant. Juan passed him a large brown paper sack and closed the door, acting as human doorstop. Salinas rolled over the doctor's chair and sat down in front of Marcos, placing the sack between his feet. Marcos took a long sip of water through a straw from a cup on his bedside table. Followed his visitor's eyes as half the liquid spilled from his mouth onto his hospital gown. It felt good.

"The last time I visited, you were still fading in and out of the coma." Marcos nodded. Salinas looked at his hands, fidgeted with his gold wedding band. "Look, there's no easy way for me to say this, Marcos." Salinas gripped one of Marcos's bony knees through the hospital gown. "Clara didn't make it. They got her to the hospital but she'd already lost too much blood."

This Marcos already knew, but it didn't stop the pain from registering on his face. He'd pestered the nurses until they confirmed the news. His last memory of her face, her smile, her feet skipping along in her youthful excitement, was at constant odds with the sound of her scream that tore through his mind when he closed his eyes. Her final moments made of loose images born from his bloody imagination. Salinas took a tissue from the table and dabbed his eyes. Crushed the dry tissue in a palm.

"The police still haven't found Eva."

Because they didn't search for her. Marcos felt an intensity rising to the surface that he hadn't felt since the day he woke up a failure. Since the day the staff told him what happened. *Kidnapped was as good as dead.*

"She's dead," Marcos said. The words, more or less, spilled out intelligible.

Salinas pulled a phone from his pocket, scrolled through screens until he found a photo.

"This was pulled from a security camera down the street from the apartment." He rotated the phone so Marcos could see. The quality was poor, but Marcos recognized the men. Not their faces—they were still a blur in his memory, but their look, their formation, he could recall. He felt his face grow hot. Five men, bathed in smoke, unleashing hell at Marcos and the girls. The throbbing in his skull increased. He held tight to the bed to steady himself.

"She might still be alive."

Juan knocked on the wall. Salinas checked his watch,

drew the paper sack out and hunched over, like a coach drawing out his final play. There wasn't much time, something they appeared to both agree on.

"Listen to me carefully, Marcos. I know who set this up, but the proof I have isn't something I can take to the authorities. The case wouldn't go anywhere and I'd be disappeared tomorrow." He stuffed his hand into the sack and pulled out a photo. "Luis Zapata, his home address is on the back." He handed Marcos the photo. "This is the man responsible for Eva's kidnapping. For poor Clara's murder."

Reduced to poor Clara. Poor, dead Clara. If Marcos clenched his teeth any harder he'd crack a molar. Juan knocked on the wall again. Time was running out. Marcos's head spun. If the man knocked a third time Marcos swore he'd lose it.

"Tonight Luis will be home; he's staying in the city and his schedule is clear. I've got you a new set of clothes, and this." Salinas held up the sack and Marcos reached his hand inside, accepting the pistol, weighing it in a shaky hand. The magazine wasn't full, but there were more than enough rounds to do the job. Marcos sensed Juan's unease as the weapon wavered up and down. The giant didn't trust Marcos, felt there was some reason he might turn the gun on the pair.

"I've talked to the doctors. They've told me your prognosis isn't good, Marcos. This is a way to set things right.

"This man will never see justice, unless we take it into our own hands. You understand that more than I ever will."

His heart whispered, *too clean, too easy.* The bullet in his brain screamed, *tonight.*

Fourteen

After Salinas left, Marcos hid the sack in a corner of the empty closet and waited until a nurse came to retrieve the lunch he'd barely touched. He'd felt uneasy since the visit, tired of the chicken soup and Jell-O combo. Salinas's words did nothing to sway him from the fact Eva was dead, her body left to the vultures until some farmer stumbled upon it on the side of the road. Another headline for the tabloids.

He tried not to think on it because when he did, all he saw were images from bruised memories of past cases. The burns, rapes and mutilations he'd come upon. Solved or unsolved, all crimes equally horrifying. A confused mix of anger and regret sat like a lump of coal burning in his belly. Made him anxious watching the minutes tick by on the wall clock that was five hours too fast. At that time, Zapata would be home, slipping off his political mask, replacing it with what? Father? Husband? Marcos didn't know the man, not personally anyway.

Marcos knew Zapata from the news but couldn't recall much detail. Just another face with GOVERNMENT stamped on the forehead. He was a career politician and that made anything possible.

When the nurse finished her checkup, he closed the IV drip and removed it from his left hand. The blood, almost black, he wiped on his gown before stripping and retrieving the bag from the closet. The nondescript dark t-shirt and jeans smelled of thrift store mildew. He fit a black ball cap gently over his head, carefully tucking the bandages underneath. Slipped the handgun into a pocket of a rain jacket before balling it up, stuffing it back in the bag. Better to conceal the weapon in case he was stopped before he could find an exit. As he headed for the door, package tucked under an arm, he paused, catching a glimpse of himself in a mirror. He adjusted the ball cap lower, shading his sullen eyes. His cheeks and lips felt like thin plastic against his fingers, irreparably soured. The face of a killer.

No one questioned him in the hallway outside his room. Those who looked up from their clipboards quickly averted their gaze. He left through the emergency exit at the end of the wing, propped open for two nurses who stood smoking outside, half a pack of smoldering butts at their feet.

He made it down the street from the hospital before realizing he'd forgotten to pocket the last of his pain meds. That, and he was already lost. The dryness in his mouth reasserted itself. *Nothing a drink couldn't solve.*

At a gas station he stood and stared at a faded map he found taped to a window until the attendant came out and told him to get lost. Marcos ignored the kid, tore the map off the building and stumbled away. Spent the last of his cash on a bottle wrapped in a brown paper bag then found a park bench, where he spread out the map and stared at the maze of roads in between pulls until it straightened itself out and he remembered where he'd been and how he got there.

After he was stabilized in Tecomàn, they flew him to a hospital in Colima with a trauma unit that could handle his surgery. The doctors and the nurses each took a turn telling him how lucky he was to be alive. It was the last thing he wanted to hear.

Zapata's address was close, less than a mile away. The location gave Marcos plenty of time to kill. He pulled on the jacket and slouched against the bench. Rehearsed what he might say to Zapata if he had the time. The heroic stuff of movies dribbled from his lips, reduced to drunken blather. He drank until his head spun, even with his eyes shut tight.

Fifteen

Marcos dreamed he lay with his head across Eva's lap. Her thighs were hard and cool against his feverish skin and when she removed his cap and ran her fingers through his hair, he felt her tears fall against his cheek. When he tilted his head and opened his eyes to see her, he found himself alone under a dark sky, raindrops pattering on his face. A throbbing pain in his skull returned as he sat up, shifting him from groggy to alert, his left side numb from sleeping on the cement bench. He pulled his watch close to his face. *7:30pm*. He'd almost missed his window. Broken glass from his lost bottle crunched underfoot. The pistol was still secure in his jacket pocket.

He walked as fast as he could command his legs to move, clutching the damp map in his hands. Out of breath before the edge of the park, he kept going; he had to. He made the distance in just under ten minutes, checking his watch again as he neared the target. Close, he took a seat on a small garbage can underneath an overhang to relax his heart. Wadded up what was left of the map and dropped it to the pavement beside him.

The address on the back of Zapata's photo was a third

story condo with a wide window overlooking the neighborhood. Marcos sensed movement but couldn't make
out any of the figures inside. Other than a few passing
cars, the block was quiet. Marcos crossed the street to the
alleyway beside Zapata's building. The fire escape looked
sturdy enough and it held steady, supporting him as he
began to climb.

When he reached the second level, the back door
on the floor above opened and a woman emerged, adding another garbage bag to a single that sat outside. It
wasn't dark yet, but the night was coming fast and Marcos had clouds leftover from the rainy season on his side.
He climbed to the third floor, took a deep breath, drew
the weapon from his pocket and opened the door into
a kitchen. He set a wet foot down on the entry rug. The
woman turned away from him with a large bowl, singing
a tune as she carefully carried it away from the kitchen
and into the adjoining room. Marcos raised the weapon,
tiptoeing after her, picturing the photo of Zapata in his
mind. His feet crossed the rug to the wooden floor with a
squeak. *So much for surprise.*

The woman screamed, dropped the bowl to the table.
Tomato soup flooded across the setting, spraying Zapata
like Marcos had already put two rounds in his chest. His
two sons, barely tall enough to see their plates, sat un-
moving in their chairs, hands locked in pre-meal prayer.
Zapata held up his arms in submission. Marcos focused
on forming each syllable but the words still came out
slow and dumb sounding.

"Is she alive?" He had to ask. It was his only chance.

"Let's just calm down a minute. Carmen, please, sit

down." The woman shook uncontrollably as she pulled out her chair and sat. The soup dripped to the hardwood floor in tiny splats. "What do you want?"

"You set this all up, where is she?"

"I don't know—"

"Eva Santos." Marcos stepped closer when he said her name. His finger within the trigger guard, poised to pull.

"Eva Santos is missing. I'm getting daily updates on the search. I'll be the first to know if we find her."

Marcos shook his head. This was wrong, this was all wrong. He'd interviewed thousands of people over the years, knew when someone was feeding him bullshit, especially under stress. The evidence Salinas had was bad. They had the wrong man.

Zapata's eyes widened in recognition. "Wait a minute, you were there. You were with her the day she went missing. The day her daughter was murd—"

BANG.

The gun bucked in his hand, a slip of anger he couldn't recall. Marcos winced as Carmen screeched. The bullet sailed over Zapata, buried in the house somewhere behind him. *Shit. It wasn't supposed to happen this way.* The boys cried in each other's arms. Zapata's hands fell to the table in shock. *He'd gone too far, couldn't take back his actions now.* Marcos took two steps back, looked over his shoulder, out the bay window, for what he wasn't sure— maybe another solution or witnesses. *Salinas could fix it. Smuggle him out of the city, back to the beach where he belonged.*

He felt a sudden sharp pain arc through his head, recognized a figure across the street cloaked in shadow.

Juan. The giant adjusted his cap, reviewing his police uniform in the window of a parked cruiser. He turned to the Zapata residence, eyes on Marcos's backlit form. Wrong man, right man—it was all a setup. Just a disposable assassin with backstory worthy of the front page that papers would kill for.

Marcos looked back to Zapata, still frozen in time, his face a mix of apology, sorrow and regret. All these things and more crashed through his mind as the betrayal sank in, but he couldn't lock down on any one of them. So instead he ran for the fire escape. Had one foot in the kitchen when Juan raised a submachine and sprayed the bay window. Carmen's scream caused Marcos to stumble, tripping into the counter, banging knees on cabinets. Heard the cries from the family but he couldn't turn back. He was on the stairs when Juan hit the kitchen, rounds ricocheting off appliances, cutting through the brick exterior.

He lost his feet on a rung near the bottom of the ladder, cracked his chin on the metal and fell onto a parked car, denting the roof. The blood in his mouth tasted as sweet as the fact that he'd held tight to his gun.

He took off at an awkward jog, his legs numb and back beaten from the fall. Needed to get away, go anywhere, but his sense of direction was as useless as the soggy map he'd left behind. He took a quick right, sticking close to the buildings as he ran. He heard a screech of tires and seconds later a police cruiser whipped onto the street, accelerating after him. Marcos fired once, the bullet sparking off the pavement in front of the car, and ducked into another alley, around a dumpster that had as much trash piled around it as it held inside. His phone buzzed in his pocket. He pulled it out and threw it as he ran. Salinas wouldn't save him.

Salinas wanted him dead.

Sixteen

Marcos held his breath, crossed to the other side of the trash-strewn alley. Started at the crack of a pistol aimed in his direction. He slipped coming out of the alley, almost falling headfirst into a passing car. The driver slammed on his horn and swerved away. More cruisers neared his position, sirens pushing him to the edge. Juan had called in the backup. Marcos let another car pass and darted into the busy street, narrowly avoiding a convertible as the driver smashed his brakes, clipped the back of a truck and spun out of control into a light pole. Another ten feet and he'd be into the alley on the opposite side.

A cruiser fishtailed a block west of Marcos, catching sight of him as he plunged into the dark alley. Shouts followed him from the street, civilians involved in the wrecks pointing out his location to police.

Marcos cut down a T-intersection. Heard the whir of a helicopter. That's when he knew Zapata was dead and he was the man marked responsible. He paused, looked down the empty alley. Every cop in the city would be descending on the area, along with the media, reckless in tow. Footsteps splashed through puddles behind him. Quickly he tried a door on the left. *Locked.* Then one further down on the opposite side. *Locked... but loose.* He dashed against it, felt something pop in his shoulder on the second try as the door crashed open and he fell inside, arms flailing, tumbling down stairs into a basement. He caught himself with his good shoulder near the bottom. Wincing, he reached down and picked up the gun, which he'd lost in the fall. He staggered upright, felt like he'd been tossed in a blender. Hid his face as three flashlights sprinted past, owners missing the stairs. Sirens whined in the distance; police expanding their search.

Marcos continued into the next room, pushing open a cheap door with a hole for a knob. He shuffled two steps into the room and stopped dead in his tracks. Had to put a hand on the wall to keep his knees from buckling.

A single bulb hanging from the ceiling cast a dim glow, adding a layer of grime to the unfinished room and hiding the corners in shadow. The cement floor was damp. Smelled of industrial cleaner with a hint of an unmistakable foul coppery smell. Near the center of the room was a wooden chair, bolted to the floor. Much of the wood was stained red. He tried to raise his pistol as he crossed the room but his shoulder screamed in protest so he kept it cocked at his hip. He mentally ran his fingers along the cuts in the wood, brutal divots in the arms and legs. Listened to water trickle in a nearby drain, stared at it as if the answers to all of his questions lie at the bottom. The secrets he'd find if he'd only remove the grate.

The feeling of sorrow that suddenly slammed into his gut was neither due to shock nor surprise at the cold scene laid out before him. He'd raided similar kidnappers' stash houses and torture rooms before and seen much worse—bodies suspended from the ceiling by their feet, severed heads stacked along the wall in neat rows like some stockroom from Hell—but they were isolated in rural locations or deep within cartel controlled territory. The fact this room was hidden in one of the wealthiest neighborhoods in the city, under the feet of politicians and businessmen, near children and their fútbol fields, left him with a chilling sense of defeat. They could be anywhere, *were* anywhere.

White light flooded the room, blinding Marcos. He jammed fingers into his left eye, pried it open to see. Fluorescent lights in the ceiling replaced the eerie glow of the single bulb. A door clicked open on the other side of the room. A man nudged the door wide with his hip, kept his back to Marcos while bending over. He was dressed in a thin see-through plastic suit that wrapped around his shoes. He hummed as he dragged a young woman into the room, the plastic zipping between his thighs with each step. They smelled of smoke. The woman's bare feet were clean, her toenails a shade of dark red. When the man neared the chair, he turned to Marcos, the remains of an empanada jutting from his mouth. Marcos let him finish the bite before he raised the gun and pulled the trigger. Recoil like a rusty blade jabbed in his shoulder socket.

He closed his eyes and took a deep breath, let the hammering echo of the shot subside. He stood over the young woman wondering what brought her to this place. She'd been roughed up, had scrapes on her elbows and knees, chipped nails. One of her hoop earrings had been torn through the lobe. She had a subtle but intense beauty about her that reminded him of Eva.

Eva...picturing her brought back pangs of failure in his chest. The woman's pulse felt low. *Drugged.* Who knew what value she held. Probably none. Just another piece to be cut off until there was nothing left. He ejected the magazine—empty. One round in the chamber. He let the gun dangle in his hand above her forehead, felt her cool breath against his fingers. Rubbed his finger along the trigger guard, slick with sweat. They'd find her if he let her go, make her suffer the same fate, or worse. Maybe her extended family next time as well. Make her watch as another stranger in a plastic suit dehumanized her closest friends, all in the name of money. The pain he could save her from. Sweat rolled off his brow, drips pattering the cement next to her face.

But...she could be the next Eva. Or Clara, all grown up. The survivor generation. Deep in his soul he found a kernel of hope, just enough to believe. He bent and kissed her forehead. Prayed he still possessed the strength for one last climb.

Seventeen

Marcos slung her over his good shoulder, used his other hand to push off the floor. The pain in his joint was replaced by a cool numbing sensation that tingled and cracked as he gripped the railing. He took the stairs one at a time, painfully slow. The night sky a deep purple mix of flashing lights through the doorway above.

Left foot, right foot.

He almost tripped twice but regained his footing. He reached the alley, exhausted. Removed his ball cap, let his head breathe. Helicopters continued their dance overhead, looping the neighborhood. He limped along the alley, used the concrete wall to help support her weight. *Almost there...*he repeated, step after step. Crowds of people gathered along the sidewalks, balconies and windows jammed with onlookers. Their intense curiosity a mixture of worry and laughter.

He pushed through into the street, police lights highlighting his struggle, illuminating his back. Voices shouting, giving and taking orders. A team of officers burst from an apartment building, crossing a parking lot, weapons drawn. Marcos stopped at the centerline, dropped to a knee and lowered the woman to the pavement. An unmarked car sped toward them, turned into a hard stop less than twenty yards away. Three men jumped out, long guns leveled at his chest. Marcos didn't recognize them, but he read their vests.

FEDERALES.

He clutched the woman's hand, giving it a squeeze. Couldn't stop his lips from forming a smile. It hurt, but it was a good kind of hurt. The kind of suffering where you get a glimpse of light at the end of the tunnel, even if it's a shade of gray.

Marcos struggled to his feet, took a step toward the men. He could count on them. He raised his arms and the first fired, then all three. He managed two more steps before he felt the strength in his legs evaporate. He hoped it was enough for a quick death. Just grant him that.

He'd earned it.

Afterword

On November 12th, 2012, Maria Santos Gorrostieta, the former mayor of a small town in western Mexico, was kidnapped in broad daylight in front of her daughter, tortured and murdered, her body found three days later by the side of a road.

An outspoken politician against the ever-increasing violence of the drug cartels, Gorrostieta had survived two assassination attempts – the first of which took the life of her husband and the second left her badly wounded. But, she continued to speak out and fight for truth and justice.

The terribly tragic events surrounding Gorrostieta's death serve as the inspiration for *Federales*. While I don't believe I could ever do her story justice, and though *Federales* is a work of fiction, I do hope it brings some attention to the never-ending struggle that is mostly out of sight, out of mind to us here in the United States.

~ Christopher Irvin

About the Author

Photo © Kimberly Rottmayer

Christopher Irvin has traded all hope of a good night's rest for the chance to spend his mornings writing dark and noir fiction. His short stories have appeared in several publications, including Thuglit, Noir Nation, and Shotgun Honey. He lives with his wife and son in Boston, Massachusetts. For more, visit christopherirvin.net.

Thank you for reading our first One Eye Press Single, *Federales* by Christopher Irvin. If you enjoy the book, be sure to leave a review online and tell your friends about this book so we can continue to publish books like *Federales*.

In fact, you can turn the page now to enjoy an excerpt from our next One Eye Press Single from crime and horror writer Bracken MacLeod (*Mountain Home*).

White Knight by Bracken MacLeod
Available June 10, 2014

WHITE KNIGHT

Bracken MacLeod

ONE

She walked into the office ahead of her boyfriend—the leash visible to everyone but her. They stopped in the middle of the room looking around for some indication of which assistant district attorney to talk to. The fading bruises on the woman's face and arms, the lingering swelling around her eye, and the scabbed lip all said that she was one of mine. I beckoned them with a finger to where I waited at the far end of the small meeting room we called "Prosecutors' Corner." The boyfriend sauntered up to the length of waist-high wall where I stood waiting to withdraw the next battered woman's story from my metal bucket full of case files. He gripped his girl's elbow and steered, leading her like a perversion of a blind man following a sighted companion. With a hint of a challenge in his gaze, he looked me directly in the eye and said, "I have a case today. My name is—"

"I know your name, Bobby," I said. Robert Hurley's face turned red as I flipped through the folders in the bucket. The stories held little suspense for me. They all read the same; only the setting changed. I'd like to say that his file was more worn than the others, but it wasn't. "No stranger to the court" is what I would call him when discussing his past with the judge while he stood listening with an equal measure of contempt and impatience making him dance from foot to foot.

Every Tuesday I met to negotiate with men who'd been gaffed up over the weekend with domestic violence beefs. The ones who weren't still downstairs waiting for someone to show up with a money order, that is. The guys that got bailed out were always the hardest ones to deal with since it was usually their wives or girlfriends who ponied up the cash to bring them home in violation of the automatic temporary restraining order. They had a list of assurances that—no matter how many times broken—were always renewed when asking for bail: "I'll do the counseling"; "I'll stop drinking"; "I swear I will never hit you again." No matter the false promise, it was always preceded by the same lie: "I'm sorry."

"Why are *you* here, Marisol?" I asked. "Shouldn't you be down in the D.V. office talking to your caseworker?" In that moment I could see into the future. She bought the lie and was here to sell it to me. I knew what was coming with such certainty that I wrote her reply in the file before she gave it.

"I want to drop the charges."

Bobby was a better ventriloquist than most; his lips didn't move when the words came out of her mouth.

"Sorry, Marisol. We've been through this. You aren't the one bringing them," I told her. "Only the District Attorney's Office can—"

"She still wants them dropped." Bobby moved his hand up onto Marisol's shoulder, marking his territory, letting me know I didn't get to tell her what was what—he did. The bruises on his scraped knuckles were jaundiced yellow, ringed in purple. Her version in the file was likely that he injured his hand when he punched the wall during their "disagreement." I imagined he might have done exactly that. As a warning before moving on to her face.

His version: *She just doesn't listen.*

"I understand that's what she said, but that's not the point. The people of the Commonwealth are bringing the charges and she doesn't have authority to withdraw them."

"But you do. And she told you—"

"You're not listening, Bobby." I locked eyes with him. He tried to give me a yard stare, but I've gotten the death glare from hard cases who actually intended to follow through with the promise in their eyes. Hurley had nothing behind his glower but a rheumy lack of commitment. I flipped up the page on the left side of the file looking for the list of arrests. "I've seen you here, what... five times since New Year's? Last winter we sent you to anger management and alcohol counseling. In February, you got diverted again with a suspended sentence of thirty days. Congratulations. That time you made it until April before being arrested for the same thing. I'm guessing you hit a lucky scratch ticket that month because you *hired* an attorney who convinced me to let you plead to disorderly conduct with more counseling and a promise to seek inpatient detox. In June, you came back for more and I see that case is still pending as we discuss this new charge."

His face was blank as a Hindu cow's as he listened to me reciting his history. He rubbed the back of his neck as if he was debating whether to go lie down for a nap or open another beer. "If she don't want to testify, you ain't got a case," he said.

I felt my face flush as Robert uttered this unfortunate truth. When your one and only witness to a crime testifies in court that "nothing happened," it's hard to meet the State's burden for even a continuation of a restraining order. The judge would know different—everyone in the courtroom would—but he doesn't have any more of a choice than me. Without a complaining witness, a judge won't sign off, and my boss won't greenlight a trial on the merits without a guarantee of a win. The D.A.'s as big a coward as Hurley, but for different reasons: he's got to massage his hundred percent conviction rate for the re-election campaign.

Hurley expected me to hand him another reduced charge like the one his overfed attorney got him last time. Then, Marisol's only offense had been to come collect him at the bar so he could sober up before a job interview the next morning. A friend told Hurley the position was practically his and they were out celebrating his good fortune—a big shot buying drinks with a paycheck he hadn't even earned yet. Marisol let him go to the interview before calling the police to report the beating she got for pulling him out from under the waitress sitting on his lap.

Counsel had gotten the matter continued and Hurley worked his way back into Marisol's graces with his bad boy good looks and a sincere tone girding his promises.

She recanted her statement to the police and the best I could do to get him to take a plea was agree to bust the Battery charge down to Drunk and Disorderly. He'd learned from my "brother at the bar" and was pushing me for what we called a "lesser included charge." And Marisol was in his corner. On his own, I could make Hurley tap out. As a tag team, they had me on the ropes.

"Bobby. Go wait out in the hall."

"Say what?" he asked.

"I said, go plant your ass in the hallway. I'll call you back in when I'm ready to deal with you." His eyes narrowed as he considered me with undisguised contempt.

"Come on, Mari," he said, turning to leave. Marisol felt the tug on her leash and stepped back from the bar.

"Not you," I said, pointing at her. "You stay."

Hurley stopped and glared at her over his shoulder, sending the message that I couldn't protect her if she chose to disobey him.

He was right.

I could see her debating who to listen to. He continued to stare her down while she searched for a way to defy both of us, remaining neutral—the position in which I imagined she always fared best. When I saw her body lean in his direction, I repeated my commands, my voice at war with his gaze. "Bobby. I'll be happy to have Trooper Gerolamo show you the way to the hall if you can't find it yourself." I opened the half door in the low wall separating us and gestured for Marisol to pass my way, saying, "Marisol. Through here, please."

Exhaling a long breath, she stepped away from her man. He watched her pass through the gate, the leash slipping from his hand. I closed the door behind her, re-pressurizing a room drained of air. Hurley knew that despite being only three feet tall, the barrier was impassible. If he tried to come for his property, Trooper Gerolamo would stop him. And it would hurt. Still, I waited to see if he'd try. Some guys only know how to do hard things the hard way.

"See you in a bit," he said, turning to leave. His shrug told me I could count on her being punished for his emasculation.

WHITE KNIGHT

Bracken MacLeod

TWO

I gestured for Marisol to have a seat in my cramped office. She plopped down in the guest chair in front of my state-issue metal desk and stared at the dead, gray screen of the TV/DVD combo on the wheeled media cart against the wall. The distorted reflection of her battered face was the least upsetting thing I'd seen on that television. While I didn't have cable, a steady stream of programming played out on it. I used the set to watch recorded statements with battered women and children. Depositions of men who somehow couldn't control their tempers at home, even though they never seemed to have a problem keeping their emotions in check when I goaded them in court. Sometimes, I played crime scene evidence tapes recorded by detectives. No matter the subject, the station was always the same: The Horror Channel.

I watched Marisol Pierce study herself in the dim screen. She brushed her fingers over the wound on her lip, lightly probing at the raised black scab before moving up to feel the swollen purple bag under her eye. She winced at the tenderness of the dark flesh there and let her hand fall back into her lap. Turning away from her reflection, she locked her gaze in her lap, staring down at fingernails she'd chewed down to the quick. Her moment of self-reflection delivered the message Hurley was psychically sending her from the hallway. Eventually, he'd know everything she told me in this room whether or not she wanted to tell him. And she'd pay for picking the wrong side.

Moving around in the cramped space to my chair, I tossed Hurley's file down on my desk and sat down. "You want to explain your change of heart?" I asked.

"Not 'specially."

"Why not?"

"What do you want me to say?"

I wondered if that's how she greeted her boyfriend on Monday mornings after she paid his bail. "I want you to tell me the truth so I can help you."

"Help me? Will you get me another piece of paper telling him to stay away? Are you going to make him do more counseling?" She laughed humorlessly. Her bitterness was well-earned. I had done those things in the past and none of them prevented him from laying hands on her again. Whether or not she bought the promises, she knew how the future was going to play out. Her life was like one mirror facing another—the same image repeating until you can't see any further down the line. But you know it goes on forever.

She looked at me with a growing incredulity that I wished she'd aim at her boyfriend. Difference was, I'd never convinced her that giving me that look was going to hurt. He had. Every single time she shot him a glance that suggested independence or opposition, she paid a cost. In her body, in her mind, in her life, he extracted a toll for every minor rebellion until there was no more fight left in her. For him, anyway. She had plenty of opposition left to throw at me.

"We both know a restraining order and diversionary programs won't do either of you any good unless you help yourself. It's time to think about moving out, Mari." The suggestion didn't even raise a spark of hope in her good eye. Her expression remained dour and impassive. Still, I tried to sell it. "I can get him remanded overnight for violating the emergency TRO. You use that time to pack a bag and come back here. We get you a bed in a shelter and from there you get your own place and get free. Along the way," I said, tapping the file, "you testify and we put him away."

"Then what?"

"Start over somewhere else. Somewhere safe." She'd never agree to it; she had family and friends in town. She had a boss who looked the other way when she came in to work looking like the loser in an undercard fight. But none of those ties were so tight that they'd step up to help her stand against Hurley.

She looked away to the wall, staring at my Suffolk U. diploma and ticket to practice. You don't need a Juris Doctor to know how the system works. Experience is a teacher. Even if she did everything I wanted and we won at trial, chances were that he'd be out in a few short months, ready to find her again. The city wasn't that big and people talked. If she stayed in contact with their friends he'd have her new number and address within hours of release. Then the program of coercion and intimidation would begin anew—first with promises, then romance, then more threats if she got too uppity, and finally another beating before the cycle reset itself. There might be slight variations in the pattern—a hospital admission perhaps—but things would continue as they had before. I couldn't promise to keep Hurley out of her life permanently unless she was willing to give up everything. And everything was a price she wouldn't pay. Not to me, anyway.

"Even if I wanted, I can't leave," she said, sighing.

"What's stopping you?"

She pulled down the drop v-neck of her sweater. I resisted the urge to leap up and fling open the office door. Instead, I held my breath and waited for her to make her point. She pulled the sweater and her black bra strap out of the way exposing a tattoo of a young boy's face over her heart. The likeness was realistic, if amateur. I'd seen a thousand back room trailer tattoos walk in and out of Prosecutor's Corner. This one was nicer than most, though marred by scabbing. Above the portrait were the initials B.L.P. and a date I assumed was the kid's birthday. "B.L.P.?" I asked.

"Brandon Levi Pierce. He's going to be six in August."

I had no record of a kid in my file. I'd been seeing her for the better part of a year—since she started seeing Hurley. The police never mentioned a child in their incident reports. And then it clicked. The Department of Children and Families had him. Must have taken him into custody when I was still 'paying my dues' doing traffic cases.

"You know you're never going to get him back as long as you stay with Hurley." The DCF's official mission statement said its focus was on preventing abuse and neglect, but under those shallow waters ran a swiftly moving current of 'preserving families' that was doublespeak for 'get the kid off the books.' They had too many children to look out for, and layoffs and 'early retirement' had left them with a skeleton crew of inexperienced and overburdened (if mostly well-meaning) caseworkers. If she wanted to be reunited with her son all she needed was a stable-looking home and a steady income stream—things that Hurley provided, off and on. She just had to make sure they were on more often than not. I wondered why she didn't already have the boy.

I played my ace card. "You go to a shelter and do the program. Testify, and I'll call in a favor I have at the Department and we'll see about getting Brandon released to you. Once you get a place of your own."

"Can you guarantee it?" She called my bluff. Her bruised face made her look tired and sad.

"Guarantee? There's no such thing. But I'll do everything I can to—"

"I want to drop the charges," she whispered. Survival. The way she knew how to ensure it.

I sat waiting for permission to breathe again. If I drew in her air, resignation would infect me. Weaken me. Leave me unable to fight. I stood up to escort Marisol back out into the hall. "You tell Robert that we'll be calling his case at nine o'clock along with everyone else's. If he wants to hire an attorney, he's got until I call his name to do it."

"But I said I want to drop the case."

"I heard you."

She stood up to leave. I offered her my card. She looked at it like I might have been trying to hand her a snake. I pointed to the number hand written on the back. "You keep that somewhere safe. Call that number when you're ready to get help. Day or night."

"And you'll come running? You're my savior?" Her voice was full of snark and derision I hadn't heard come from her before. I saw then what she really thought of me and my promises.

"I'll come," I said.

"I won't hold my breath." She flung open the door, letting the knob bang into the wall, and walked out of my office making a show for the secretaries of pulling up her bra strap and sweater. For a second it felt like seeing the desert reappear through a shimmering oasis letting me know that shade and water weren't in my future. As soon as she got to the wall, the mirage shimmered back into view and she dropped her head, shuffling through Prosecutor's Corner like a whipped dog.

WHITE KNIGHT

Bracken MacLeod

THREE

I called Hurley's case last, making him wait on the hard oak pews until nearly one o'clock just to stand up and say 'not guilty' and pick a date to return to court. If it hadn't been a light morning, I would have made him wait until after the lunch recess. It was a petty thing to do, but sometimes the process is the only punishment. Marisol stood next to him, holding his hand and whispering her answers to the judge's questions, making Hisonner ask her to repeat each statement loudly enough for the court reporter to hear.

After the arraignment, I went out front to have a cigarette with Trooper Gerolamo on the courthouse steps. I watched Marisol Pierce ride by, sitting in the center of the bench seat in Hurley's pickup truck. From the Smokers Lounge, I could see the son of a bitch was gripping her shoulder so tightly his fingertips were turning white.

"You can't win 'em all."

"When have I ever won, Gerry?"

Made in the USA
Lexington, KY
26 March 2014